Joseph Caldwell, Walker Anderson

Autobiography and biography of Rev. Joseph Caldwell

First president of the University of North Carolina

Joseph Caldwell, Walker Anderson

Autobiography and biography of Rev. Joseph Caldwell
First president of the University of North Carolina

ISBN/EAN: 9783337118075

Printed in Europe, USA, Canada, Australia, Japan

Cover: Foto ©Raphael Reischuk / pixelio.de

More available books at **www.hansebooks.com**

AUTOBIOGRAPHY

AND

BIOGRAPHY

OF

REV. JOSEPH CALDWELL, D. D., LL.D.,

FIRST PRESIDENT

OF THE

UNIVERSITY OF NORTH CAROLINA.

By order of the Editors of the University Magazine for 1859-'60.

CHAPEL HILL:
JOHN B. NEATHERY, PRINTER.
. . . .
1860.

AUTOBIOGRAPHY

OF

REV. JOSEPH CALDWELL, D. D.

AUTOBIOGRAPHY.

The Edict of Nantes was revoked by Louis XIV about the year 1684. The well known consequence was that 500,000 French Protestants left their country to look after settlements among other nations, and in other parts of the world, where they might enjoy the rights of conscience, and the same immunities and prospects for themselves and their families as were common to other subjects or citizens of the governments under which they should live. One of these emigrant families was that of Lovel. They first passed from France into England, and continued there for some time, in the exercise of manufacturing skill. At that period, the colonies of America, now known as the United States, were fast filling up from different parts of the British empire, and Europe. The head of this Lovel family did not continue very long in the vicinage of London, before he concluded to transplant himself with such capital as he possessed, which, it would seem, was not insignificant, to a spot which he selected on Long Island, towards it western extremity, and not far from Hempsted Plains, and near Oyster Bay. Here he purchased an extensive farm. The land was of good quality, and being faithfully cultivated, yielded annually an abundance for the necessaries and comforts, and all that was desired beyond these for the enjoyments and respectability of people who classed with the substantial mediocrity of the country. With what total abstraction and absorbing interest did my good old grandmother, when I was a boy of twelve, sit and pass in review through the details of her early years, while she was growing up under the fostering guidance of her venerable parent. He was, it would seem, of mellowed affections and patriarchal habits. I shall give a specimen of one of these conversations:

GRANDMOTHER. My father was considered a man of strong mind. His person was large, his expression tempered of gravity, affection and truth, on which the eye rested with confidence. He was often cheerful in aspect and intercourse, but he was always under the chastening influence of piety. He had learned to understand the doctrines of the gospel through the stern constructions of Puritanism, as it has been distinctively called in England. In France, people of this description went under the name of Huguenots.

GRANDSON. Huguenots! That's a strange name. Why were they called Huguenots? What is the meaning of it? I suppose it is some nickname, by the sound of it.

GRANDMOTHER. It probably was. But I do not know its origin or its meaning. They were persecuted so cruelly that they escaped out of France by thousands, to find subsistence and settlements as they might in other countries. My father and his connexions got to the sea coast and went over into England. They were people of property. Some made purchases of houses in London, where they died without heirs. We were told of this some time afterwards, and might have inherited the property, but my father was either unable or too regardless of the matter to attend to it, and time ran on until by the statute of limitation the claim was barred. Some have said that even now, if the claim could be clearly substantiated and conducted through the forms of law, a large number of houses once belonging to my uncle might possibly be recovered by our family, and if they could, we should all be rich enough.

At this I remember that my little heart bounded, and I became full of inquiries.

GRANDSON. Well, Grandmother, why cannot that be tried? Is it not worth while? You say it was a vast property, how may houses were there said to be?

GRANDMOTHER. I have heard of a considerable number. My uncle was a bachelor, and is said to have owned a whole side of a square, consisting of valuable buildings.

GRANDSON. Has any attempt ever been made to recover the property? If not, would it not be well to make a trial at least, and, if it should fail, we should but be where we are.

GRANDMOTHER. Yes, my child, if there were anybody to do it. But it would imply a great deal of trouble, and time, and expense, and it has been thought best to give it all up.

This was a theme on which I delighted to dwell, with the fond idea that if all that property could be reclaimed, it would be the consummation of our good fortune.

GRANDMOTHER. After my father's emigration to this country with his family, he brought up his children to the habits of industry, piety, and economy. But though he held the reins of domestic government with a steady hand, a spirit of harmony and affection was constantly diffused through all our feelings. We stood in awe of our father, and feared to transgress, but it was accompanied with such a confidence as to strengthen and deepen our love for him, and was attended with a prompt and willing acquiescence in his wishes. Our mother, too, seemed to look up to him with such deference to his opinions and wishes as showed that she felt him to be her guide and protector as well as the partner of her bosom. One singularity that marked his feelings and opinions was that he never suffered meat to be eaten in his family.

GRANDSON. Not eat meat! That is strange. I never heard of any body that never eat meat. What reason could he have for not eating meat?

GRANDMOTHER. He was wont to tell us that the grant to live upon the flesh of animals was certainly in the scriptures. But he considered it to have been made in consequence of the fall of man. Hence, he deduced that to abstain from it was more in conformity with original innocence and perfection, than was the practice of subsisting upon it. He never permitted an animal to be slaughtered for his own use or that of his family. He always had large and luxuriant pastures, kept numbers of cattle and such other animals as could be useful to him upon his own principles, provided plentifully for their sustenance and shelter, had an abundance of milk, butter, cheese and fruits, wheat, corn, and vegetables. In short, all around him, both in the house and in the field, was in the best condition.

GRANDSON. But, if he sold one of these animals to be killed by another person, would not that be much the same thing as killing it himself?

GRANDMOTHER. So he felt, and he never would consent to sell one if he knew it was to be slaughtered. Some animals we keep now without ever thinking of killing them for food, such as horses, dogs, cats. He put all upon the same footing.

GRANDSON. But, Grandmother, you eat meat now, and your family were all brought up to it.

GRANDMOTHER. Yes, but I never tasted it till I was married, at 21 years of age. Your Grandfather had no such opinions and habits, and I fell in with his customs and those of his family. To the present day, however, I care very little for meat. My father and all his family were thought as healthy as any people in the country, and seemed to enjoy themselves as much. We were apt to be esteemed peculiarly happy among our neighbors—always harmonious, plain in our manners, affectionate, looking up to our parents with veneration and love, and prompt acquiescence in their wishes. We were taught to be scrupulous in the economy of time, and to feel unhappy unless we were busy about something useful. We had a family library and were educated to an enlargement of the mind, by reading and improving conversation. My father was careful in directing the habits, dispositions and intelligence of his children. Their ingenuity was continually called out for the accomplishment of such work as was assigned to them. If a difficulty occurred, the answer to an application for aid was, "Now try your skill. Is there no way you can contrive for effecting what you want? The greatest advantage in your doing that, is in finding out the best method." This would interest us in our work, and if we succeeded, we were applauded and encouraged, and this gave us fresh heart for our occupation.

GRANDSON. Why, Grandmother, you seem to have been very happy

GRANDMOTHER. We were usually so. My father was fond of sacred music. He brought over an organ with him, and kept it in his family. He could play upon it himself and sang well—at least we thought so. Most of my brothers and sisters learned from him in succession as they grew up. At the hour of morning and evening prayers, the family all assembled in the room where it was kept, and united their voices with its elevating tones in praising God. It is the very same organ which your uncle John Lovel has in his house, and on which you have heard his sisters play, who are now living with him.

Such were the accounts which my kind grandmother would detail to me of old Mr. John Lovel, her father, and his peculiar habits, opinions, and mode of life in his family. It can scarcely be supposed that I am professing to describe these things in the expressions used at the time. In the course of my boyhood, they were renewed at different times. They were subjects on which I delighted to hear her converse, and they made indelible impressions upon me. The circumstances and events have been here given in such terms as have occurred.

As there is something curious in the events of this family, I shall go on to mention some of them as they arise in my memory. One of my grand-aunts married a man by the name of Wright. They lived in Philadelphia, unhappily, I was told, for he became a sot, and she was a woman whose pride, it would seem, was not a little towering. When she saw her husband thus degrading and brutalizing himself, she felt the mortifying effects in all their force. After his death, she resolved to continue no longer in the city, and planned an expedition for herself, which few women would think of carrying into effect. She took passage in a ship for London, with such property as she possessed, declaring in the loftiness of her spirit, that she would throw herself upon the resources of her genius, determined to seek eminence in a different sphere. She took lodgings in the city of London, and began with tasking her invention to devise some scheme of eminence. I know not the different methods she might have thought of for accomplishing her purpose, if more than the one by which she in some degree succeeded employed her ingenuity. Her name came before the public as the inventress of the art of making waxen figures of full size, with a strict likeness of the persons for whom she took them. This implied more art and skill than would at first appear. The material was to be purified in the first place, and, if the object required it, be brought to a perfect whiteness. It must then be mixed with some substance that would give to it the proper complexion. It must not be liable to become soft by any temperature of the atmosphere, nor be liable to crack by cold, after being formed into a shell of no great thickness. Her mode of taking a likeness was different, as I am informed, from that which is now practiced. I believe that waxen figures are now made by first forming a mould of some other material, and then casting the wax into it. She chose an apron of some fine stuff, such as cambric, and having so prepared the wax that it should be sufficiently soft to yield and spread with the warmth of the hand, she gave it a first rude shape by holding it in her hands and moulding it rudely with pressure applied at discretion, while, as a portrait-painter, she looked at the countenance and consulted the visage and features she would imitate. She then placed it under the apron and brought it to the perfection she wished by acting with one hand applied to the interior of the waxen shell, against the other on the outside with the cambric between the hand and the surface. This gave it a natural aspect, by exhibiting the pores of the skin, and prevented the glazed and cadaverous appearance of which most persons complain in such wax work as we commonly see. Her faces had the reputation of being not only striking likenesses, but of being natural in expression and agreeable in effect.

This invention was new, I was told, both in bringing waxen likenesses to the full size, and in the whole manner of producing them. From being totally an unknown personage she rose into notice, her name was regarded with distinction, her resources became ample, and even the court treated her with favor and respect. Something of the effect which it had upon her I have had occasion to remark from letters written by her at the time to one of her sisters, Mrs. Willis, in America, in which she often inculcated upon her the favorite maxim by no means to fail "in maintaining the dignity of her character." It was even curious as being sometimes interjected with as little connexion with the subject as Cato's *"Delenda est Carthego."*

Sometime after this the American war commenced with the Declaration of Independence. Aunt Wright, it would appear, was an ardent Whig, and not inactive in her country's cause against the measures of Great Britain. She engaged in political matters, and acted the part of a spy, for which it is probable every American will not respect her the less, by writing letters to some of our leading characters, giving information of the measures of the British Government that the Americans might be on their guard and prepared for events. In this she was at length discovered, and orders were sent to her to leave the kingdom. She passed across the country with a view to embark at Bristol. While there, walking in the street, she made a misstep, fell, and her ankle was so much injured as to terminate in mortification and consequent death.

My aunt Wright left two daughters—to one of them, by the name of Elizabeth, she bequeathed the greater part of the wax work. This had grown to be extensive by continual additions in London, where it had been kept for exhibition. It was transported to New York, where it was set up by my aunt* Betsey, in spacious rooms, to which all visitors were admitted by the payment of a quarter of a dollar each. I was then a boy living in Elizabethtown, sometimes at Princeton, and sometimes at Newark, getting my education in the academies of these places. Aunt Betsey had married a man by the name of Platt, who was a trifling character, and who persecuted her much. She at last became scrupulous in regard to the correctness of keeping waxen figures for exhibition, and her conscientious feelings upon the subject disturbed her so much, that she resolved to part with them. The figures were numerous, the drapery was often rich and costly, and the whole workmanship had at length amounted to no small expense. She determined, however, to get rid of it, and sold it at a reduced price. This happened at the time of my arrival in North Carolina. I remember the feelings I had on the occasion. I was then young, had traversed alone a wide interval to place myself among strangers and in circumstances wholly new. I saw the wax-work which was carried through the country, it being at that time a perfect novelty to the public. I had often seen it before in New York. It seemed as if when I looked on those lifeless figures they fell little short of raising in me the fullness of those joyous transports that spring up in our bosoms, when, in a land of strangers, we suddenly turn our eye upon former acquaintances, or upon friends near to our hearts. My aunt had come to think it a profanation for her to set up those figures and likeness of the dead for show. I could not suppress a revolting indignation at the thought of the degradation and disgrace which they suffered in being carried about the country to be shown in taverns and to tasteless people, who knew nothing of the events and associations with which they were connected in my bosom, who were unqualified to feel or estimate the merits of the work, the characters and circumstances exhibited, or the skill necessary to the production. Some of those figures might be considered as emblems of fallen greatness. They had been among the first works of the kind in London. They had directed upon them something like the admiration which men feel for original genius. They had even received the visits and fixed the eyes of the most refined courtiers. Now, they must be officiously introduced and studiously recommended to the most debased subjects that crowded common barrooms, or who surpassed but little the animals they bestrode.

My grandmother's maiden name was Rachel Lovel. She married a Mr. Harker, who was a minister of the Presbyterian Church. What was the extent of his education I know not, though there is reason to think it was respectable. It is likely, however, that he had not been originally

---

* Or Cousin?

given up to a literary course from his first boyhood. It is more probable that he commenced life with manual labor, and that it was not till he was advanced towards manhood that he undertook to study for the ministry. He settled with his family at a place called Black River, in Morris county, New Jersey. His residence was on the edge of a hill along which the public road lay for nearly a mile. His house was a mile from Flanders, a pretty village, so called because it had been remarkable for quarrels and violence in the first settlement of the country.

I was told that my grandfather Harker was remarkable for personal size and strength. By this circumstance, combined with vigorous mental faculties and fidelity in his profession as a pastor, we may account for the opinion, said to have been prevalent, that the people in that vicinage looked to him as their leading character in counsel and in action. He was experienced in all ordinary practical business. It was said of him that he would go into the harvest-field and cradle more wheat in a day than any other man in his part of the country. In his ministerial labors, both in and out of the pulpit, he was ever regarded with high estimation and confidence by his congregation. Their feeling was, that in the lot which had fallen to them of having him for their minister, they were a flock that enjoyed the privileges of a vigilant and faithful shepherd, able to counsel them in their secular interests, and to guide them to a better world through the embarrassments, trials, and conscientious struggles of the christian warfare.

My mother's name was Rachel. She married early in life, a physician, who was also young, and just commencing practice. His name was Joseph Caldwell, whose father had emigrated from the northern part of Ireland. Of three children I was the youngest. My brother's name was Samuel, and the difference of our ages was almost exactly four years, for we were born in the same month. The birth of a sister intervened, but she died very young.

I have been informed that my father never admitted that he was correctly treated in the provision made for the children of the family. There was property, it seems, but none was left to him. His father was professionally a farmer, who looked to his children, as they grew up, to assist him in the support of his family and the enlargement of his property. My father was of a more delicate system than the rest of the children, and with this peculiarity united a taste for study and mental occupation. On this account he was no favorite with my grandfather, who estimated his children chiefly by their efficacy in advancing his wishes. He was slighted therefore, and by no means gratified with desired opportunities of improving his mind at schools or academies. To this he was obliged to submit till he arrived at an age when he was able to help himself forward by becoming useful to others. He struggled through his difficulties into the medical profession, and probably his father thought that as he had contributed nothing to the making of his estate, he ought not to think himself aggrieved if he was left without a share of it.

He contended vigorously with his difficulties, and was successfully rising in his profession. But, as he was alighted one day at a mill either having accidentally stopped, on being expressly solicited on the emergency to aid, he joined the too small strength that was present in replacing a mill-stone. The force which he exerted was too much for him, he ruptured a blood-vessel in his lungs, a profuse hemorrage instantly followed, a rapid consumption was the consequence, and in a few months he sunk into the grave. The death of my father, his burial, and my birth followed one another in the order here mentioned in three successive days. It was impossible, therefore, that my eye could ever have looked upon him. The woes of that period to my excellent mother must have been felt by her to have reached an awful consummation, through alarms often renewed, hopes disappointed, and sorrows protracted for months before the dark and trying events in which they terminated. She was still in early life, and just at the season when the prospects of her husband, herself and her commencing family were brightening, a terrible cloud, dark and dense, suddenly settled upon them, at length fell with sweeping violence, and after reiterated assaults left my poor mother, widowed with two orphan infants, prostrate and powerless amidst a scene of desolation.

My father died on the 19th of April, 1773, was interred on the 20th, and I was born on the 21st, at Lamington, in New Jersey, near Black River, a branch of the Raritan, a mile from old Germanton. My father's remains were deposited in the burying-ground annexed to the Presbyterian Church near that place, as appeared by the inscription on his tomb, which I visited a short time before leaving that country to become a resident of the South.

What were the circumstances of my mother through my infancy and for some years afterwards, it is of little consequence to state, if I knew them. I have some early recollections that spring up in an insulated manner, but how they succeeded one another, it were vain to give any account. I have not the vanity to suppose, while I am writing this account of my life, that any part of it is to be thought worth the time necessary to its perusal. It is for every one to do with it as he pleases. Should the wish to know occur to any one, he has the opportunity of such reminiscences as are sufficiently distinct to be ascertained in what the writer sincerely intends to be a register of truth.

The date of my birth, it will be observed, makes the earliest scenes of my life cotemporary with the Revolutionary War, or with events immediately connected. I remember the calling away of men from their homes to serve in the armies, and the spirit that was manifested in the countenances, conversations and actions of people around me. The marching of troops, a circumstance which I always hurried out to gaze on with sensations rising almost to transport; the fife's shrill and piercing notes, stirring into reckless activity emotions of which I had scarcely known myself capable; the drum rattling into madness every impetuous feeling that thrilled along the nerves or swelled in the heart; the plumes and epaulettes of the officers; the measured and stately march; the burnished arms, the extensive columns presenting the movement of a vast and powerful body pervaded by one animating spirit—all made impressions upon me at the time which in some of their characters may be considered as peculiar to the years in which they were produced, and which therefore could never have been attained, but at the period when they were actually acquired in the experience.

At one time I was under the care of my grandmother at Black River, on a farm left to her by her husband, the Rev. Mr. Harker, at his death. She was far advanced in years, and I extremely young. Her kindness, as is usual in such cases, is in my recollection, but there is reason to think that my misconduct was too much for the total suppression of her feelings. Both she and my mother were ever faithful in giving me all the instruction in their power, and especially in training me to the knowledge of God, of the scriptures, to pious sentiment and religious duties.

One night, alone in bed, I well remember being occupied in my thoughts almost to solicitude on our manner of breathing; and the next morning the first question I put to my grandmother after seeing her, was, how it was possible for us to breathe in the dark? I do not know whether this was an inquiry involving too much for her philosophy, or for my supposed capacity of understanding such explanation as she might have been able to give, but no answer was returned, and it was not till many years afterwards that I found the solution of my difficulty.

My grandmother would sometimes, though I believe not often, become much vexed with my behavior, and when her anger was roused, the emphatical expression that she uttered with a shake at once of the head and hand was, "*I'll break you.*" This threat, understood literally by me and not in the figurative sense in which she used it, was to the last degree terrible. It presented her to my imagination as placing me across her knee, and snapping me in two, as she would dry sticks or a pipe-stem.

We lived in the neighborhood of a man who took great delight in terrifying children. I would sometimes wander in quest of amusement, till being near his house, he would suddenly present himself, writhing his muscles into all the distortions expressive of fierceness, his eyes flashing with rage, and his motions indicative of the most desperate purpose. It never failed to inspire me with an instinctive promptness for flight. The effect was a complete panic, and precipitated me into so intent an economy of time, that to have incurred a loss of it by looking over my shoulder was felt to be perfectly inadmissible, and in such cases I never discovered the distance which had been widening at every step between myself and the enemy, until I was fairly within the threshold of my grandmother's door. I relate this little circumstance, to show how some minds will prefer that kind of gratification which arises from making themselves objects of terror, though accompanied with the utmost detestation, before the pleasure that springs from communicating happiness even to children, and being the objects of their love. It was not long before I left that seat of my earliest years, and it never failed to return upon my recollection as a little paradise, but the corner of it, to which this man was contiguous, seemed ever haunted by a demon with whom abhorrence in my imagination was inseparably connected.

At another period of these earlier years, my mother lived in Amwell, a part of the State to which I believe she had retired from the confusion and exposure of the warfare near Elizabethtown, New York, and other parts of the maritime country. While we remained here for two or three years, my memory had stamped upon it much of the agitation and discussion that prevailed respecting the proceedings of Congress, of the States, of Great Britain, the armies and battles, the raising of militia for short service, and the enlisting of troops during the war, the successes and disasters of the contending forces. One fact continues vividly in my recollection, that a man of our neighborhood, in respectable circumstances at home, who had served with the militia, suddenly made his appearance among us after an absence of some months, barefoot and his clothes hanging around him in rags and tatters. I looked upon him with astonishment, and probably with the more, because I was totally unable to comprehend at that age, the possibility or necessity of his being in such circumstances.

We afterwards lived in Newton, and then in Trenton, but in the latter of these places not till very near the close of the war. While we resided at the former, a body of men arrived from the American army and the scenes of its active movements. Newton was the court house village of Sussex county, and high in the interior of the State. Dates I cannot recollect, but it is not improbable that it was at the period when the conflicts were going on in lower Jersey. While I was mingling among these men, one of them gave me a fife. I went home in ecstasy, but great as it was, it was doubtless not more exquisite than the annoyance was to others, as I soon had occasion to learn; though I could by no means comprehend how my notes should not be as enchanting to them as they certainly were to myself.

At a subsequent period, young Symmes lived at Newton, distinguished afterwards for the theory which he wished to establish, that the earth was a hollow sphere, and that the interior part was accessible near the poles. His father had married my mother's sister, so that we were cousins german.

When my mother lived at Trenton near the conclusion of the war, the portion of my life which passed at that place has ever recurred as unequalled in interest by any other in my recollection. Our situation was exceedingly pleasant on elevated ground at the southern limit of the town. The distance was but small to the bank of the Delaware. Being then about 9 or 10 years of age, it was my custom to stroll as far as the river. The prospect up and down its expanse was always enjoyed with exquisite delight. Above were the falls, where the river dashed, and roared and foamed among thickly scattered rocks, displaying a scene of incessant action, animating at once to the eye and the ear. On the opposite bank was a mill almost always in motion. There the current of travellers passed by a ferry, on the principal route between New York and Philadelphia. Below was spread to the eye a long reach of the river, passing the village of Lamberton, otherwise called Trenton landing, where such masted vessels and other craft as were fitted to the navigation, were seen in motion, or presenting a scene of activity at the wharves.

The banks and fields were covered with verdure of a velvet softness. A refreshing coolness was diffused through the limbs by the shade from above, and the earth through its grassy carpeting. A smooth margin of composted sand between the bank and the water, diversified with its pure whiteness the beauty of the scene, while the spirits were quickened into gaiety, by the light motions of the numerous birds, by their shrill and varied notes, and by the fish that often bounded wholly above the water, or sported upon the surface.

It is hoped the reader will excuse this indulgence of a lightness, if not puerility of recollections, which have often recurred through the successive years of a life, much indebted to them for their cheering brightness, when interspersed, as they often have been, through scenes of more grave and sombrous aspect, and connected at last with the present approximation to its close.

One of the latest events of this last residence at Trenton, was the wintering of a body of troops, on a beautiful field, separated from us only by the public road leading to the ferry already mentioned. The interest of this circumstance was much abated to me by their being French, in consequence of which, though I was often permitted to stroll among their tents through the day, I was cut off from every attempt at communication with the men, or of learning any thing from their conversation. One of the impressions most deeply engraved upon me, was from the nightly calls of the sentinels, which I scarcely ever failed to hear, at whatever period I happened to be awake, through some months of their continuance in that encampment. Though it was a mere formal hail, with the inquiry briskly addressed. " Who goes there ?" and the answer, " Friend," yet, upon my ear it never failed to strike with a stirring and portentous sound. One day as I stood near the door looking towards the river, my eye was caught with a sudden gleam, and was almost as quickly directed to the spot from which it proceeded. Two men appeared fully in view on an ascending ground, beyond a small ravine, engaged with rapiers in furious combat. The sun was shining with all the splendor of a clear day, and the glittering of their swords seemed to convey, as by an appropriate language uttered to the eye, the flashings of their rage. I stood in momentary expectation to see one or the other sink before me with a fatal blow. Such were their eagerness and their quickly renewed passes at each other, and yet so prolonged was the combat, that I became petrified with horror that grew upon me till I was almost overpowered, and I believe I turned away for relief, for I certainly did not see its termination. I soon inquired, however, and was informed that neither of the combatants was killed. Two officers, who were friends, had taken a walk, and began to amuse themselves by stopping now and then, merely to try their dexterity in fencing with their swords. At length, it seems their feelings became too ardent for mere sport, and finally mounted to mortal fury. The difference of their manner was apparent. Both were skilful ; but one never retired from the footing that he took, while the other, with a sudden thrust, instantly bounded off from his adversary who almost as speedily followed with another thrust in return. I was told that the one who had practiced the elusive movement, had not succeeded in the strife equally with the other, for he had received several wounds, and began to be weakened with the loss of blood, but had inflicted scarcely any injury of consequence. The action was witnessed immediately at its beginning from the camp, a file of men was dispatched, and before any fatal mischief occurred, they were put under arrest.

I think it some time after this, that my mother removed her residence to Bristol, a place lower down the Delaware, and on the Pennsylvania side of it. Here I went to an English school, which has always returned upon my remembrance with peculiar pleasure. I believe the reason of this was, that the master had an excellent talent for exciting good dispositions in his boys towards himself, and to their studies. The affection I felt for him has never been extinguished to the present day, and I have no doubt it would continue unchanged to whatever number of years my life might be protracted. I was never kept to closer diligence in business, and yet my heart reverts to it as among the most interesting and happy periods of my life. Here I first engaged in the study of arithmetic, and though I found much perplexity in some parts of it, which would probably have created aversion under some teachers, I returned to every effort with fresh determination and courage. This feeling seemed to be inspired and maintained whenever my eye was turned upon the man. He was ever intently occupied in the various business of a numerous school; was prompt and dextrous in every thing; his expression was that of kindness and a wish to improve us to the utmost; and, as this was apparent in his features and his actions, a corresponding sentiment seemed to be transfused into the bosoms of his pupils, carrying us at once into a concurrence with his wishes, and an efficacious improvement of our time.

But a circumstance which most impressively marks this period is, that here I began, for what reason I know not, to turn my thoughts with greater earnestness than before, on the subject of religion. A part of the time while I was in this village, my mother went abroad leaving me to board at a neighbor's table. This was so near that one of the rooms in the house which she occupied, was left open for my use both day and night. Here I slept, and whenever I chose, to this I retired. I got hold of a religious book, and finding it give me pleasure in the reading, young as I was, and fond as most boys usually are of play, though I was much at my own discretion, I would sit or traverse the room alone, reading with an interest that grew so as utterly to preclude every disposition to stop.

While I was living in Bristol, an incident occurred which might have had some connection with this subject, though it had certainly happened so long before this disposition to religious thought, that in my reflections since on that part of my life, the one circumstance has no appearance to me of having induced the other. On a Sabbath my mother was absent, having left my brother and myself at home. She had always made it a particular point in our domestic education, to pay a strict regard to the faithful observance of the day. I strolled down to the wharf for amusement, and while there, my brother and another boy came down, and a very small boat lying at the place, he immediately got into it to go out upon the water. I immediately became eager to accompany him, and urged for his permission. This he refused, but while he was at the head of the boat I sprang down upon the stern. My weight was not much, it is true, but the descent being some four or five feet, and the boat small, the impetus sunk the end on which I alighted some distance down into the water. It instantly mounted up again, and as I was in a toppling condition, and unversed in humoring the motion, I was tossed overboard and sunk, I know not how many feet, to the bottom. The pains of death of course commenced with the first expansion of my lungs, and they produced the utmost efforts of such action in all my limbs as nature prompted, for I knew nothing of swimming. Though I was very young, my reflection was all alive to the thought that a few moments were to end my existence here, and send me into another world where my destiny was to be forever fixed. The anticipation was horrible, and my struggles were convulsive. The distress both of mind and body was complete; my thoughts were hurried, but they were distinct; and it may well be supposed that no words can give utterance equal to their intensity. After a while I found myself approaching the light. Having by my struggles risen to the surface, I found myself prevented from sinking once more, which, had it occurred, I have no doubt would have ended the strife. My brother had placed himself at the spot where I went down, and as it happened, I at last rose so near that he caught me by the hair and saved my life.

When I was lifted out of the water and placed upon the wharf, I found myself surrounded by a number of persons, who had hurried to the place. The water spouted from my mouth and nostrils for some time with renewed efforts, until I began to feel relief. My sensations of joy for the deliverance of which the moment before I had been utterly hopeless, were as exquisite and indescribable as the horrors I had suffered. What a vast transition of feeling, and in how brief a space! It is a species of knowledge, which in its peculiarity and extent, is probably unattainable but by the actual experience. Though I was obliged to be supported or carried up to the house, a flood of pleasure even to exultation was pouring through my mind, not apparent, as I think, to others; but not the less real in intensity and continuance. I was given to the repose into which my exhausted powers naturally sunk through the afternoon, and when I awoke it was to see my mother gazing on me with concern. At once shame and self-reproach must have been the expression that met her eye, for they were felt in all their force. I was dumb before her. She saw that it was enough for every purpose she could wish, either of warning or reproof; and so tender was she to my feelings, if not wholly engrossed with gratitude for my preservation, that for a long period not a word escaped her lips in my hearing, even to impress upon me lessons on the subject, which she probably saw there was no occasion to illustrate or enforce. For this I loved her the more; for though I was quite young, I ascribed her forbearance to what I have ever since believed to be the real cause : that she could not bear to lacerate me, when the wound upon my conscience was probably almost too deep for my fortitude to bear. I had been guilty of disobedience, but this was not the most aggravating circumstance. It was on the Sabbath, and I was violating it by going in quest of amusement wholly at variance with the reverence with which she had ever taught me to regard it. If she had inculcated upon me that what had happened was a judgment from God upon my transgression, it would have been unnecessary, for with this impression it already rested upon me in all its force.

These feelings gradually faded from my thoughts, and I lived as heedlessly as ever. It was long afterwards that the pious affections of which I have already spoken, became quickened in my bosom, nor am I conscious that the event just related had any connection with them. I was left in solitude at the time, and taking up a religious book, I began to read—my feelings were excited by it, and they grew into ardor and intensity. I deserted all amusement, my reading, my reflections, and a gratifying sense . that I might be engaged in the service of God, and have his approbation, abstracted me from any of the diversions that occurred to my thoughts. As to the cause, it was perfectly inexplicable, and always has been. My experience at that time was probably one of the first fruits of the pious sentiments which my mother had instilled into me from the first dawnings of reason. She was not there, but the spirit of God was doubtless fostering these principles in my heart, and educing them into action. I have since reverted to the few days which passed in these circumstances, and with these emotions alive in my bosom, as among the most grateful seasons of my life, and ever to be remembered with renovated satisfaction.

It could not have been long after this, that we removed to Princeton. Here all the circumstances and events of my life begin to appear less severed from one another by parts wholly forgotten, or obscurely remembered.

Here was a grammar school, and from the interest which I had been thought to show in reading books, my mother was counselled by others finally to adopt the measure which herself had meditated, of giving me a liberal education. The difficulty most felt by her, was the want of such an income as would sustain her in the undertaking. I think it was in the year 1784, when I was eleven or twelve years of age, a Latin grammar was wanted, and upon inquiry none was to be had. We waited some days for a supply, but none came; and as the determination was made, I grew impatient. One of the boys by the name of F—n from Charleston, being told of the circumstance, and having one on hand that was nearly worn out, gave it to me. I refused it till I was told that he had two. I always felt grateful to him, and through the whole time of our acquaintance in the school, for three or four years, he manifested a peculiar friendship for me. The grammar was instantly and eagerly commenced, and as eagerly prosecuted till finished. Corderius, Selecta e Veteri, Selecta e Profanis, Cæsar, Greek Grammar, Greek Testament, Mair's Introduction, Virgil, and perhaps some other books, followed in as quick succession as intent application could compass them. Before my entering college, our family removed to Newark, where my studies were continued under Dr. McWhorter. The school at Princeton was made an object of special regulation, and sometimes of personal attention by Dr. Witherspoon. From this circumstance it certainly had singular advantages in comparison with other academies. The modes of instruction, and the exercises in which we were trained, were derived immediately from Scotland. Of their superior efficacy I was made sensible by the change. Dr. McWhorter was undoubtedly among the best teachers in the country, but in the class with which I was united, every thing came so easily in my preparations that it was almost like sport, while the rest of the class appeared to meet as much difficulty as they could well vanquish. This difference proceeded from the different methods of teaching, and I was perfectly convinced of it at the time.*

While living in Newark, my religious impressions were often renewed. I do not know that I resisted them, or strove to repress or shake them off, but it is very certain that at various times when they had been felt with much force, alarm of conscience, and a dissolving tenderness of affection, they soon passed away, and I became as careless and thoughtless as ever. Dr. McWhorter's preaching was generally animated, plain, and practical. He sometimes became warm, pointed the guilty sinner to the coming wrath, showed the danger of growing hardened to all the considerations of God's mercy, his justice, his judgments, the means of grace, the opportunities of improvement, the uncertainty of life, and the dread consequences of failing to prepare in this time of discipline and probation for the eternity that is to follow. I would come home like the wounded hart with the arrow in my side, but it dropped off, the wound closed, and it ceased to be remembered.

---

* For instance, in Mair's Introduction, it was the custom at Newark to write down no more than two or three of the longer sentences in good Latin, as a weekly task on Saturday. But in Princeton we were required to come prepared every forenoon, while we were in that book, to read the whole of one of those sentences in English, and then to repeat it with equal promptness in correct Latin ; and our daily appointment was two or three pages. Nor was this all. For we then closed our books, and the instructor would read to us long portions of the English, and we must give the Latin of them without mistake in word or grammatical construction, from beginning to end. We were not permitted to do this tardily, for not only if any one made a mistake, but if he did not move directly forward in enunciating the translation of the sentence put to him, the next below was to pronounce it forthwith, and if successful, was to take his place. To a student trained to this vigor and promptness of thought and action, what difficulty could there be in writing down two or three sentences in corrected Latin as a weekly exercise, as was the custom at Newark? We wrote Latin versions weekly at Princeton also, but we had nothing but English sentences given, and we selected the Latin words and phraseology for ourselves. This taught us the use of words agreeably to their true classical import. Dr. Witherspoon had various methods of drilling a class. One was to run a verb,

That our present life is a state of trial, I think must be confirmed by
every man who reflects upon the events of his own, and the manner in
which they affect his mind, his affections, his outward condition, his mental character, and his prospects of the future. Limiting our views even
to our earthly existence, it is probationary. Our choice of action, at any
moment when it is made, must be regulated by the past, that we may
choose our object, be intelligently directed to it, whatever it may be, and
that the means may be adapted to its attainment. In regard to every one
of these we are liable to error, and of course to be corrected by experience.
This experience constitutes the very thing which is called providence by
those who believe in God's administration of all human affairs. It sets
before us all the variety of ends which it is possible for us to choose, and
we are subjects of trial, when we make our selection. If our end be a
good one, it is one evidence in behalf of our virtue. We have been put
to the test on this point, and it has terminated in our favor. If we limit
ourselves to instrumentality which God approves, it is another proof that
our affections and views have been formed as we have advanced through
the past upon correct principles. If conscience has been our authority, it
is still further testimony, by evincing both that it is enlightened, and that
we have listened as became us to its voice. If at any time we have not
adhered to these principles, it proves no less that we have been in fault,
and as we have had our choice, we must properly sustain the consequences.
One great consequence must ever be, that if we have chosen ill, and re-
fuse afterwards to be chastened by its external effects, or the reproofs and
interdicts of the heart, we give proof that we are, so far at least, ripening

---

as it was called, through all the successive tenses and moods in the first person, then in the second person, the third, and so on: and to repeat the impera-
tive, the infinitive, the gerunds, supines, and participles. This was done in
both voices. Another exercise consisted in comparing an adjective, and keeping up the repetition of the degrees, through all the genders and cases in both
numbers. A third method of giving us skill was to carry an adjective through
the cases and numbers in company with a masculine substantive, then with
a feminine, and then with a neuter. A fourth exercise was to come prepared
daily with a page or two of vocables, so as to give the English for the Latin,
and the Latin for the English. In another instance, he would select a Latin
verb, and call upon each of us, successively, to give a compound with the meaning, till all the compounds were exhausted. A sixth exercise was made out
by taking some verb, as *ago*, having various idiomatic imports according to its
connection, and we were required to give examples of its idiomatic uses. This
note is subjoined evidently not for all readers, but as a suggestion to teachers.
But these are by no means all the methods of drilling to which we were called.
When we first commenced any one of them, we were slow; but the quickness
to which we presently attained, was evidence of the improvement consequent
upon such practice. The most efficient cause of the high degree of perfection
at which scholars arrive in European grammar schools and scientific institu-
tions, is to be seen in the diversity of exercises devised and continually practiced through the whole course of education.

in iniquity, and exposing ourselves to God's disapprobation, to that of all good beings, to our own, and to all the calamities which God has connected with it, in the constitution of his works, and by his positive determination. If it be said that we are the children of circumstances, still it is true that these circumstances are at once the arrangement of God, so as forever to retain us under a complete responsibility for the result as to good or ill which is to be their issue with respect to us. If we cannot choose our condition, or control events, we have our choice of the course we will pursue, so far as sin or obedience to the truth is concerned. This is unquestionable at every step we take, we have the incontestable evidence to it, which is of the nature of fact, the evidence pronounced by consciousness, whenever we appeal to it. The overruling power of the Almighty, then, detracts nothing from our complete responsibility. We are truly and justly probationers, both in our present state, and as to our framing ourselves to the good or ill connected with our welfare or our misery hereafter. He gives us external opportunity of knowing our duty, and having it forcibly urged upon us. He impresses it upon us by his Spirit, in a manner calculated to reform and improve us. This he never would do, were we, who are of wicked dispositions, not in a state of trial, nor susceptible of recovery. Were not this our condition, were we not in a state of discipline and responsibility, but wholly given up to the spirit of disobedience which every man feels to be prevalent within him, our only feelings at all times would be opposition to holiness, and complete abandonment to its motives and the outward expressions of it—our universal intercourse—and a consequent utter despair of heaven, and an overwhelming sense of final consignment to sin and all its woes.

I have indulged in these reflections here, because they are the result of the thought and experience of all those years of my life on the events of which I am now turning a reviewing eye. I can remember many occasions in those early years, in the various places in which they were passed, when my reflections were directed on God, a future state, and the eternal world. The interest I took in them when they were impressed upon me by the scriptures, or by any other cause, was the same in its aspect and species as it has been through later years. The intervals sometimes are apparent as to their cause, and sometimes they seem to have become irrecoverably lost to my remembrance. Whether they had a connection with one another, and by what ties of circumstances, or thought, or emotion as they were successively renewed, it would be impossible for me to determine, though to the Spirit of God who produced them and witnessed all their effects, they are present now as at the moment when they agitated my bosom. Sometimes I would return from church with a heart deeply affected with the considerations presented there of my obligations to God for his goodness in the ordinary blessings of food and raiment, relations and friends, health and the pleasures connected with it. Conscience impressed upon me portentously the consequences of my thoughtless ingratitude. The prospects of heaven to the good, and of endless misery to the wicked, drove from me for a time every wish for the amusements on which I was commonly intent. The love of God in sending his Son into the world to redeem me from death, and open the way to heaven, combined with all its force in impressing my conscience with the responsibility imposed by this consummation of mercy. My mother was often engaged in giving me religious instruction, and deepening its impressions upon my heart. Sometimes an accident would happen, to set before me the utter uncertainty in which I lived. The death of a neighbor by sickness, or by some sudden accident, the grave-yard, the darkness of night when in solitude, naturally accompanied with abstraction from sensible scenes, and plunging my thought into the spiritual world—every thing of this nature excited in me a sense of religion, a reference to God, and to the danger I was in of being lost forever, if I should die without being made the subject of his saving grace. It was all the striving of his Spirit, to prevent me from being wholly engrossed with the earth, and to educate me in this school of his providence for better and more glorious purposes than the interests and pleasures of a mere earthly existence. An excellent practical writer on "Keeping the Heart" remarks that "Providence is like a curious piece of tapestry, made of a thousand shreds, which single appear useless, but put together, they represent a regular and connected history to the eye."

I am reminded here of an incident which happened at Princeton, but which it did not occur to mention among events there. Among our boyish diversions, it was one to range ourselves in two companies, and having small wagons, to run stages, as we called it, along the street, to see who could pass and leave the others behind. One day we set out in this manner fresh and buoyant in our spirits, six in each company, and pressing the strife of our opposition to the utmost. We presently met a wagon with four horses, and in turning out, we all took the same side of the way. Our company, as it happened, were to pass between the other and the team before us. Our antagonists, thoughtlessly urged to take advantage of the circumstance, suddenly thrust themselves against us as soon as we came by the side of the horses. In the instant six of us were all thrown in a promiscuous heap directly upon the track of the wheels. It happened that the driver was following his wagon at some distance behind, and could do nothing in the emergency. The animals it seems chose their steps so as not to strike or trample on any of us. The wheels were to come next. The movement that overthrew us was so sudden and unexpected that I had no knowledge of our situation on the ground, and I was so completely under the rest that I could see nothing. In thinking immediately afterwards upon the matter, it appeared to me most natural that I should have waited till the others might have time to rise and release me; and this was my first thought after I was down. But it continued only for a moment. The very next instant I commenced a violent effort of limbs and body at hap-hazard, contracting and tossing in every direction, so as to disengage myself with a speed that quite surprised me, when I considered the confining pressure which had seemed to forbid all hopes of extrication. By this exertion, those that were above me were thrown off, and no sooner was I released than I sprang upon my feet, and found myself outside of the road, but in such confusion of senses that I knew nothing of the imminent danger I had eluded. I saw, however, the fore-wheel and then the other pass over the ankles of one of my companions. The rest had been saved from being crushed by the same effort which had proved the means of my own escape. The petrifying and awful effect, however, which was produced upon me, may be conceived when immediately afterwards I was told by a boy who saw the whole, that while I was down my neck lay exactly across the route in which the wheel was to run. I was young and thoughtless; but the first reflection that rushed upon me, was, that God in his goodness had saved my life by prompting me in the critical moment to act as I did. I exchanged not a word more with any one, but walked home with feelings sunk as low as a few minutes before they had been elevated. I soon found that every one but my mother knew the circumstance, and they seemed to gaze at me for a time with particular interest. My resolutions rose to a high pitch of strength, that I would no longer live as before, in the neglect of my religious duties. My mother afterwards learned from others the peril in which I had been, for I could not bear to tell her myself. She remarked, as did others, that a deep and settled gloom hung upon me for many days, and my feelings were certainly in accordance with their observation.

There are doubtless incidents in the life of every one, which cannot but appear calculated to produce religious impressions. Even the man who is habitually an unbeliever in a special providence, will probably remember some, if not many, which had their instant effect in filling his mind with thoughts of God, of eternity, and a want of preparation for passing out of the present into a future state. If this be true, it is evidence of the nature of fact, that in our constitution we are destined for immortality. The first references of our minds in instances of danger, or extreme distress, are the language of nature. They may, in after thought, be resolved into baseless notions and superstitious fears, but still it must be admitted that our first suggestions are those of religion, and bear all the marks of being the genuine result of an original determination, to us inevitable, and as certainly natural. Is it to be esteemed a privilege or an honorable distinction to be wholly exempt from them? Then the brutes, in this respect at least, are to be envied by us, for whatever other attributes may be common to them and us, they are most unquestionably devoid of the religious faculty. For my own part, if there be a possibility, ascertained by the actual experience of any one, of a real and total freedom from the apprehension of future responsibility, and the consequences of conscious guilt through past life, when pressed by sudden peril upon the verge of death, it is a peculiarity in which I have never participated, and of which, therefore, I am unable to judge. To meet death with unyielding firmness in a righteous cause, or in inevitable necessity, is not incompatible with the gravest consideration of its ultimate issues. To unite these in our feelings is not only honorable, as something of which the inferior animals are incapable, but constitutes one at least of the most glorious distinctions of man among rational and immortal beings.

My recollection tells me that I have always been susceptible on the subject of religion. This has been the case on occasions of public or retired worship calculated to excite pious reflection and devout emotion, as well as in instances of sudden peril. It is not remarkable, however, that examples of the latter description should have taken the most tenacious hold upon my memory, both on account of their rare occurrence and their deep impressions, and the peculiar vividness of the emotions excited by them. That they were directed in signal mercy, I am perfectly convinced, both from the nature and permanency of their effects.

While at school in Newark, it was usual for us to bathe in the Passaic. On one of these occasions, my companions commenced amusing themselves by running along the ridge of a high sand bank, and jumping from the extremity down a precipice of five and twenty feet, taking care to present their feet in alighting in such a manner as to sink them into the sand that lay loose and sloping in large quantities near the bottom, so as to be stopped gradually by its easy resistance as it was carried before them. I observed their manner for some time, and was prevented at first from attempting it by the height, and the danger of not preserving the right direction of the body and feet through so long a descent. At length, however, I resolved to put it to the trial, and the very failure happened which I had apprehended. They had commenced with small distances, till learning the manner to be consulted, they at length bounded from the top almost to the base. The essay with me was through the whole extent at once, and throwing out my feet too far, I alighted upon the extremity of my body with a shock that struck me breathless. It was attended also with so agonizing a pain in my back that I had no doubt it was broken, and that it must terminate in immediate death. I had perfect presence of mind, and made some attempts to breathe, but wholly failed. The torture was extreme, both of body and mind. At length I felt cheered by some commencing success, and in about five minutes I found myself able to rise upon my feet. The pain abated afterwards in a manner that perfectly surprised me, and once more I seemed to have been snatched, as in a moment, from the jaws of death. My companions who had been appalled at the accident, were rejoicing over me as we walked home, which I at last found myself able to do, though it was at least a mile from the river. Once more I was for some time oppressed with a melancholy feeling at the thought of the danger I had escaped; but I am ashamed to say, that it was accompanied more with the pleasure of safety, than with gratitude for the deliverance, or with steadfast resolutions to live prepared to die.

While I continued in Newark, my progress in the languages was uninterrupted. I never experienced any thing like reluctance or dissatisfaction in relinquishing amusement for study. I do not know that I was ever whipped for not getting a lesson. My usual feeling was that of gratification, when the hour for reciting arrived. The consequence was, as may be supposed, and as all my recollections suggest, that my teachers and myself were mutually satisfied. And though I have seen much of the indisposition of youth to prosecute knowledge when it was put into their power, and they had nothing else to do, I have never had such a comprehension of aversion from it, as their experience would probably convey. Nor is this by any means to be supposed singular. In every school or literary institution where numbers are assembled, there are always some, if not many, of whom the same thing is true. Yet, we are compelled to believe that there are others, if, indeed, they do not make the majority, to whom it is equally mysterious, how it is possible so to delight in study, as to have their richest enjoyments broken up, if they could not be employed in it.

Having been much engaged in the instruction of youth, it has sometimes occurred to remark to such as could not be induced to an improvement of their opportunities, that there were hundreds of minds to whom, if the avenues of knowledge and its enjoyments could be thrown open as liberally as to them, it would be estimated as a consummation beyond which there was no earthly privilege, which, even in their youthful imagination, they would be so visionary as to have a conception of or a wish for. Upon some, perhaps, a beneficial impression has been left by the thought; but upon others there was every reason to know that it was followed by no other feelings than those of offence and irritation, which they would unhappily deduce from a supposed, or at least a chargeable, invidious contrast to their disadvantage between themselves and some others who were far beneath them in the world.

We at length removed from Newark to Elizabethtown. At this place too much time was lost to me in advancing my education. I believe all thought was for some time relinquished of extending it further. My time passed away in such boyish amusements as casually offered, or my invention contrived. After a year or two had passed in this manner, which I cannot but consider as wholly wasted as to all important acquisition in knowledge or culture, Dr. Witherspoon, who had known me in the grammar school at Princeton, passing one day in the stage through Elizabethtown to or from New York, mentioned to my mother the subject of continuing my education. He encouraged her to do so, if it could be effected, and he dropped some hints that if it could be no otherwise accomplished, himself would become my patron and see that by some means I should be sustained through a collegiate course. When he was gone, I was told of it, and in a moment, though I had nothing before me at home but an unlimited swing in pastime, my heart bounded at the suggestion of renewing the prosecution of my studies. My recollection presents to me no influence of motives springing from the ultimate consequences of a liberal education. The engagements of a school had always been interesting to me, and it was the gratification that was to be renewed, that filled me with eagerness for the object. I therefore teazed my mother with inquiries respecting the precise manner in which the Doctor had spoken of the matter, and the probability there might be that my studies might be resumed. Some weeks, if not months, passed away in .this uncertainty, and at last I received information that the determination was becoming conclusive in my favor.

Before leaving the subject of my residence at Elizabethtown, a circumstance occurs as having furnished another instance of the manner in which Providence decides our destination through life by incidents upon which the future seems to turn as upon the nicest pivot. In traveling along a road, the difference may appear of little import as to which of two roads we may happen to take when they are presented to our choice. The region we are to traverse, may seem to be much the same, especially to our early youth, which knows not how to look at distant consequences. And yet, by the decision made at the moment, the whole scenery and circumstances of our future days may become totally different from such as would have ensued had the determination been different. While living, then, at Elizabethtown, my mother spoke to me one day of a thought which had entered her mind of putting me into a printing office, to be brought up to that business. After asking the particulars as to the manner of making provision for it, and the man with whom I was to be placed, I was captivated with the plan, and urged it with much persuasion to as speedy an issue as possible. It would seem that I felt no real complacence in the

4

idle life that I was leading, nor any wish for its continuance. The occupation of a printer was connected with literary pursuits, and my education was sufficiently advanced to enter upon it with advantage, and to furnish a foundation for an enlarged and liberal prosecution of the profession. Such were my views, even at that early period. Every day I asked my mother how the plan advanced, and when I was to begin. She told me that she had proposed the matter to one who carried on the business and published a newspaper in the town, that he had promised to consider it, and was to give an answer. At length she received one in the affirmative: but no sooner was it reported to her, than she revolted from the project, and informed me that her mind was now in such a state that she never could consent to it. At this I was not a little surprised. I argued, and even remonstrated: explained to her the comprehensive prospects which I hoped to push with success, beyond the mechanical parts of the profession, that I had no idea of limiting myself to humble and contracted views in the business, and that though it was easy to do this, it was with a view to the ulterior and higher opportunities it would put in my power, that I was induced to wish for it. When her dissent was communicated to the one who had consented to take me, he complained not a little, and I urged this also as a reason for concluding the affair by letting me go to him. All, however, was of no avail. She had thought more fully, and could not be reconciled. Her reasons on which she conclusively rested, did credit to her sentiments, whether those reasons were in accordance with fact and truth or not. She finally objected to the profession, as having a tendency to harden and pervert the heart, by engaging it in the temptations and wiles of controversy. The facility of publication to one who commands a press, she said, was a snare, inducing him to give vent to passions, and to commit himself in sentiments, which, if sustained, must injure his moral principles, and, if relinquished, must expose him. It seemed to her as if a familiar and mechanical dealing in types was attended with the consequences of recklessness and hardihood in regard to true sentiment, as sailors who eminently live in the midst of dangers are most regardless of conscientious restriction, and learn to "sin as with a castrope." It was with such impressions as these, whether experimentally true, or only baseless apprehensions, that she explained her purpose as it became finally settled on the subject, and the plan was relinquished. It was so long after this that Dr. Witherspoon proposed the continuance of my education through a complete collegiate course, that the thought of my becoming a printer, from which I had been so critically diverted, had dropped out of sight. But when I look back at these events, they contain to me a striking exemplification of our being wholly at the disposal of Providence, while at the moment we may think of nothing else than of determining every thing by our own choice, or by the opinions and wishes of our friends. This conviction is more apt to be made upon us, when on the turning point we took a direction that changed the whole aspect of our life, than in cases of minute and scarcely observable consequence. But there is no difficulty in seeing that by one of these two, or by a succession of them, we may come to be placed in circumstances equally decisive upon an extensive scale, or in producing such a contexture of our character and condition at last, as must exhibit those little events or influences to have been of the utmost consequence, though while they were passing they scarcely attracted our notice, and have long been forgotten, and become to us as though they had never been.

Had the bestowment of me upon the printer been fulfilled, the whole train of circumstances and events ensuing upon it must of course have been different from the course into which the disposition by Dr. Witherspoon gave a direction. The time came when the conclusion was announced to me, and that the stage was forthwith to carry me to Princeton. It was in the spring of 1787, and I was fourteen years of age. A few hours brought me to the place, but they were filled with a profusion of thoughts, as to the immediate and more distant prospects that were now opening before me. The course of trial already past, of the species of employment before me, was of such a nature as not to harrass me with distrust, and though at an age when we may be supposed to feel but little concern about the subsequent years, still distant, when the arrival at manhood will call upon us to act for ourselves, my anticipations then extended to them. The tender premonitions which my mother had sometimes poured into my bosom, while the tears flowed down her cheeks, she would cast her eye forward, and endeavor to impress me with the dreadful uncertainty of the course I might choose, and the destiny that awaited me in the world, had not been wholly lost upon me. I had long been idle, and in the habit of looking for nothing but pastime, but this occasioned no regrets, and I looked forward to assiduous application as the certain and proper consequence of the change. Upon this my purpose was fixed, nor was a doubt felt that it was to be instantly and constantly realized.

On arriving at Princeton, I went and offered myself to Dr. Smith for examination, and being told that it would be proper for me to see Dr. Witherspoon, I went to him at Tusculum, a mile in the country. He subjected me to trial on one or two sentences in Mair's Introduction, and then said that I must enter the senior class in the grammar-school. This was a mortifying disappointment to me, for I had counted on joining the freshman class in college. I did not realize the effects which a long absence from studies had produced, and when called on to make Latin, rushed upon it as though I had just left it off. I instantly experienced the consequence, in the tardiness of my recollection, and the blunders I committed. I told the Doctor I hoped soon to renew my attainments, which had been much impaired by long intermission, and that if allowed to enter the freshman class, I should prove able, by a close application, to take standing with it. He replied that even if I could, it would be under so great disadvantages that it was by no means advisable; that I was young, and that he wished me to have every opportunity of being a good scholar. He said that by taking a stand upon entire equality with my classmates, I should, by a sense of strength, go on with pleasure in the prosecution of my education, instead of being disheartened by difficulties, and liable to have the standard of my feelings lowered, and of becoming reconciled to inferiority, by resorting to the reflection that I ought to be excused on account of my disadvantages. The Doctor was unquestionably right, for though my feelings suffered mortification at the moment, I never doubted afterwards of the solid benefits resulting from his determination. As it was, I was graduated under nineteen years of age. Of what importance was it to finish an education sooner? And even had my years been such at the time, as to have brought on a completion of my collegiate course at one, two, or three and twenty, instead of nineteen, the consequences of laying a substantial foundation, of growing into proper confidence and decision of character, by habitual success through every occurring difficulty, and the greater maturity of faculties by the delay, would have been amply sufficient to recommend the retrocession of a year at the commencement of the course.

In the autumn of 1787 my class became freshman in college, and at the end of four years afterwards we were graduated.

A residence of four years and a half at that time of life, may well be supposed among the most interesting of all that I have ever passed. It is usual for men liberally educated to remark, though certainly it is not without exception, that the collegiate part of life is often an opportunity of experimental comparison, more happy than any other at least of equal length. As it happened with me, the impression is confirmatory of the truth of the remark. It was not, however, without deduction in ample sufficiency to do credit to another conclusion which men have been apt to pronounce when life is drawing to a close, that when the whole with all its diversity of coloring, is looked at with a retroverted eye, it is questionable whether the enjoyment or the suffering has predominated.

When a concurrence is here expressed in the opinion that the years of a collegiate life are among the happiest we ever enjoy, an explanation seems necessary to prevent mistakes of most pernicious tendency. Whatever may have been the experience of others, my own tells me that if any instances occurred, and my recollections sadly remind me there were some in which I sought after enjoyment in violations of the laws, it was not to these that I have ever held myself indebted for that portion of time which was to be credited as happy. If there was any pleasure in the moments of clandestine acts of mischief, it was so mixed in my bosom with the agitations of apprehended discovery, and dread of the consequences darting across my mind, that I should be far from recommending it on the score of enjoyment. But in all such cases, and I most heartily thank the guardian Providence that was over me that they were not very numerous, as soon as they were over, the gloomy cloud which they brought upon my feelings, and which they kept hovering around me for many days, was enough to decide most unequivocally that much was to be set down on the page, not of profit but loss. Things of this kind which I did during the four years of college residence, were happily "few and far between," so that the effects produced in each instance in tormenting me, had some opportunity of fading out of my recollection, before another could act with any temptation upon me. But the miseries more or less, which in compliance with solicitation, I sometimes consented to inflict upon myself, were only a portion of the consequent suffering. They have never returned upon me but with pain, and always to beget most sincere wishes that they had never happened. Then with the sensations from which they have sprung, have been their unfailing retribution, when they have been resuscitated in my remembrance.

Undoubtedly it were well if all who have lived in colleges were similarly affected by similar causes. We have occasion to hear persons reverting with no small amusement, if not with delight to the disorders committed by them while students of college. It is true, there are sports of a description to be recollected and related without regret for any ill in their nature or their consequences. But every act at variance with the laws or the regular business of a body of youth assembled for education ; especially such violations as spring from a spirit of insubordination, opposition, or ill will to instructors; all schemes of mischief by night or by day that have for their object to produce tumult, disrespect towards the persons or the authority of teachers, or to dissolve energy in the prosecution of business by diffusing levity, or contempt through the transactions of it, can never be re membered by a man of correct feeling without compunction and chagrin.   And if these be the sentiments excited in the bosom, the feats in which they were exhibited must drive out all the pleasure that can be supposed to proceed from the renovation in our bosoms of the lawless and pernicious hilarity which was once permitted to revel in our early years, at the expense of all that was valuable in the habits, dispositions and attainments of our primitive education.

I have sometimes seen persons advanced in life, manifest no hesitation in recounting by the hour the disorders of their college life, in the presence of youth, and even of their own sons, who were themselves students at the time, and passing a vacation at home, or incidentally in company with them at the very site of the college, or perhaps some other place. The manner, the loud laugh, the arch and contemptuous jeer at the instructors upon whom, their tricks, if not their gross and shameful outrages, had been directed, all acted as a charm upon the thoughtless being in whose hearing they were recited with so much glee, and he would return into the college, charged with a spirit of mischief, and with a disposition to beard the faculty, or his tutor at least, up to the very brim. What consequence is so likely to be heard of next, as that the young man has become a bad member of his community, that he is remarkable for idleness and dissipation, that his time is passed in furtive acts of disturbance, noise, interruption of others, sallying out in the night upon excursions of intemperance, debauch, and such heroic deeds of irregularity as will serve to fill up hours of transport in the recollection, to the delight of the company around him in future years. But these are not all the consequences of which he may expect to hear. The most probable result is, that the youth may present himself at the door of his parents, to stun their ears with the intelligence that he has been ejected from the place of his education upon one or more charges of ill behaviour, so violent as at once to make it impossible for him to be retained any longer in the college, or so incorrigibly persevering that all attempts to reclaim and save had been exhausted upon him in vain. Then commences another process no less dangerous to principle, if it can be made successful. It consists in presenting the picture of the wrongs, oppressions and prejudices of those with whom he had to deal, in such coloring and form, as to win upon the affection to which he appeals, turn over the ignominy of the case to the authors of this foul treatment, and thus be initiated in the methods of commencing with ill, and triumphing by address. It is infinitely better never to speak of the disorders of a college life, whether once committed by ourselves, or reported by others, but with the most decided disapprobation. This is preferable in all society, but especially in that of the young. Let such disorders never hope to find countenance or palliation with those who wish all the guaranty possible to the prospects of their children, or to the efficacy of good education in the country. Too many are apt to indulge the weak imagination, that to expect or insist that a youth shall refrain from disorderly or rakish practices, would be to make him miserable. The better method is to impress him with a conviction, and rationally and affectionately to make it, as far as we can, the true and internal result of every experience, that every escape from temptations of this nature is to be estimated as an escape from the miseries inseparable from a corruption of the heart and degeneracy of habit.

Nor let it be thought, that when a youth strays from a regular deportment, he is to have sentence harshly pronounced upon him as though his
case were highly penal. The difference is wide between displacency on
our part in their extravagances, and an imputation of total abandonment.
But through the whole range of this interval, while we are confining ourselves within it, we may still feel a portentous gravity towards their follies,
show earnestness in the connection of their mistakes, frown upon
their excesses, and pronounce with severity upon their transgressions. In
doing all these pertinently, we need never be afraid that we are detracting
from their enjoyments by withholding them from immoralities, but for
our encouragement feel most confidently assured that just in proportion
as we can become successful, we are building up and establishing their
true instant as well as permanent happiness.

I have been led through these reflections by a recurrence to the events
of my collegiate course. Their importance to the young, to parents, and
to society, it is hoped may apologize for their protraction. Through the
whole of that period of my life, my habits were marked with diligence,
punctuality, and good will to my teachers, and the habitual satisfaction,
I believe I may say enjoyment, which is the natural conseqence of these.
To this an exception must be made in an event, some circumstances of
which it may not be amiss to relate. Toward the latter part of the time
that I lived in college, it became customary for the steward to furnish a
milk diet alternately, with coffee at supper. At length it was observed
that our supper table was served with bread and milk only, and it came to
be understood as a rule finally adopted that nothing else was in future to
be expected. Numbers were dissatisfied, and the discontent soon spread
until it was supposed universal. This was signified to the steward, but it
produced no alteration. The feeling grew to a higher pitch, and it was
resolved that measures must be taken to obtain redress, as we thought
proper to call it. The method seemed to us moderate enough, for it consisted in nothing more than entering the dining room in the utmost order,
in the usual manner, taking our seats regularly, and in forbearing to touch
the food. This we continued to do for some two or three days, at the
supper hour. We begun at length to grow tired of it, and as it seemed likely to continue, the students became violent, and when the door was open-
ed for admission, threw in a volley of stones, which, as the tables being
long, stood with their ends towards the door, raked them, as mariners
would say, fore and aft. The whole, as is obvious, was a foolish piece of
business, but the last was most unwarrantable, and ought to have been too
shocking to be perpetrated except by a vulgar mob. Certainly it was unworthy of a society of young gentlemen of the first order, as we professed
to be. Could we all have been transferred back to the grammar-school,

there would have been no perplexity in selecting a penalty fitted to the nature of the act. But under the system received in colleges, we had doubtless made good our claim to the credit of posing the Faculty as to the method of treatment best adapted to the emergency. To give way before violence and outrage, especially with combination, was not to be entertained for a moment. The difference between coffee and milk was a trifle in comparison with the consequences to the government of the institution. We were told that Dr. Smith would personally attend at the table with us in the evening, to take his supper with us, and observe the quality of the milk, against which complaints had been raised. This was a new thing, and as we certainly had a high respect for his person and character, it was to be tried whether this would not be enough to bring us back to propriety. The experiment failed, for, while the vice-president and tutors took their meal, the students touched nothing.

I find, however, that in reciting these pitiful details, I am engaged in matters that may well be supposed to become sickening to the reader, as they do once more to myself, and as they always have done whenever they recurred. And yet I have known many an insurrection raised in a college, the merits of which were not more respectable than this. The following day, it appeared that our offences were felt to have risen to such a height, that the Faculty could not reconcile themselves to the ordinary transaction of business with us, and our recitations were broken off until the order of college could be restored, and respect to the authority and laws re-established. The general feeling now showed itself agitated and tumultuary and, as is usual in such cases, stories began to be circulated, either totally groundless, or distorted into provoking shapes from some little fact or expression wholly indifferent in its nature which might have actually occurred, but all ingeniously and strangely calculated to excite the reigning resentment especially against the steward. And now we continued to be tossed for sometime in a manner to most of us more and more distressing, while others evidently exulted in the pretext it furnished them for every species of disorder, and the protection from punishment, under the plea that the best students of the college were involved alike with themselves. It was not very long before that which the wisdom of the Faculty had hoped and anticipated, really happened. Most of us began really to wish to find out some mode of extricating ourselves from the perplexity which continually grew more painful and embarrassing. This was probably soon understood by Dr. Smith, and many of us rejoiced when we were told that he would be willing to see a few of us in his study. A number were speedily selected, and I happened to be one. We presented ourselves before him, and he spoke to us at once with gentleness and a dignified reserve. He asked if the students were prepared to come to an understanding with the Faculty upon any terms which could be consistent with the re-establishment of authority and the government of the college? I well remember the shameful manner in which some of us met this inquiry. And I among the rest assumed to talk swellingly, and to endeavor to show with what wrongs the students had been provoked, particularly by the steward. But I have done with the narrative, when it is further said, that we took care not to leave the Doctor without accepting the assurance he gave, which was that if we were all prepared to submit to the laws of college, and return to order, it would be acceded to on the part of the Faculty, and the business of the classes might immediately re-commence, without further notice of any thing which had been done. It was a grace on the part of the Faculty, which some of us were very far from having a right to expect. For my own part, without any disposition at this moment to extenuate any absurdity in which I was implicated while that shameful behaviour was going on, I was certainly not forward in participating in the disorder or promoting it. It is enough for me, and ever has been, when the remembrance has haunted me, to think of the bold and flippant airs which I assumed in that interview with Doctor Smith. To these I was very much prompted by my standing before him as a representative of the students; for as to myself, my feelings and conduct were habitually respectful, benevolent and ingenuous. But the plea with which I then sustained myself has never since that period been able to mitigate the bitterness of my mortification, or prevent the ardent wish that my conduct on that occasion could be merged in a complete and perpetual forgetfulness.

I have already related some incidents from which I narrowly escaped with life. Another of this nature happened, while I was a student of college. It was usual for us to resort on summer evenings to a particular spot in a small stream about a mile distant, where the water was deeper than common, to amuse ourselves in bathing. A sort of raft had been constructed by nailing planks to cross pieces of timber of no great size, so that a surface of plank was made on both sides of the pieces. It was not very buoyant, and would scarcely bear the weight of one individual without sinking under him. The sport consisted in hanging around it by the hands, thrusting it about, and turning it over in the water. Several were engaged in this manner, and the amusement became so inviting to me, that though but just beginning to swim, I felt persuaded it would not be difficult to keep myself above the water by means of the raft. I watched my opportunity and reached it, but no sooner was this effected than it was turned into a vertical position by the rest, and the next moment came down and covered me as under a trap. I was instantly drowning, and again began to think myself wholly lost. Happily, one of
5

the company perceiving that I was gone and no more made any appearance, pushed away the raft from above me, observed where the air made its appearance that was escaping from my lungs as they filled with water. Being well grown and strong, and I but small and light, he seized my arm and bore me to the shore.

Rescued once more from those dying agonies, I ought to have been filled with gratitude for the mercy which had spared and preserved me. But these feelings had at the time but little place in my bosom. Through the earlier part of my residence in college, religion found scarcely any admittance into my heart. It appeared to be a subject of which I had become exceedingly thoughtless. The studies to which I was daily called, the amusements of athletic exercises, of walking through the fields and into the country, the pleasures of growing knowledge, the occupation of castle-building, to which my imagination was much addicted, the gratifications of success in my recitations, interspersed with occasional failures, calculated to mortify and vex me, the pleasures which I took care generally to secure, of success in the public examinations, the buoyancy of spirits which immediately followed, seeming almost to lift me up from the earth, from a sense of release from every restricting tie of business, and the opening of a vacation of some weeks' continuance in unlimited freedom, constituted altogether a series of occupations that left no time or disposition to think of God, the giver of all my blessings, of the sinfulness of my heart, the uncertainty of life, or the prospects and destinies of eternity.

But I was not left to proceed uninterruptedly under this engrossing influence of the world. In the full enjoyment of health, I attended breakfast one morning as usual in the steward's hall. It was customary to supply our table with buck-wheat cakes, which being light, well made, and bespread liberally with butter, were counted by many of us, at least, among our luxuries. I had heard it suggested a little before, that those cakes were prepared upon extensive copper surfaces, for the purpose of greater expedition. No attention, however, had been paid to the report. It was heard as an idle story, which some might propagate to discredit our fare. After having eaten about half a breakfast, my eye was caught with what I thought a pretty lively appearance of greenness upon the cakes, of which I had been freely participating. A sudden horror thrilled through my whole system. In a moment a full conviction seized upon me that I was poisoned, and that I was beginning to feel the fatal consequences. I rose almost tottering from the table, asked permission to retire, and from that instant through the space of several weeks, considered myself as hastening speedily to the grave. Never did an unhappy being continue more harrassed and agitated from day to day with symptoms of dissolving strength and a rapid decline. I sometimes suspected, for I wished to think that I was under mistaken apprehensions of having received poison with my food. But though it did not fail to occur that others ought to have been affected similarly to myself, it was impossible with all the efforts of which I was then capable, to shake off the impressions that haunted me, that various feelings to which I was subject, indicated a hastening dissolution. A dismal melancholy brooded over my mind, as a dark and lowering cloud. My whole aspect and manners must have soon appeared altered to others, though I had an extreme reluctance to let my situation be known, and strove much at first to carry a countenance of cheerfulness, for which I was usually rather remarkable. My spirits were depressed. The world grew to be a matter of indifference, or rather unpleasant repulsion. I could think no more of it as having interests for me. I involuntarily retired from intercourse, and courted solitude, that I might be free to indulge in the gloomy train of reflections that kept me miserable. I often prayed that I might be prepared for death, but derived no satisfaction from it, for I seemed to be sunk down and lost to all the capacities of happiness or hope.

It is probable that others observed and distinctly noted the change that had passed upon me, long before I suspected them to know or think any thing respecting it. It appeared as if I was shut up within myself, and had ceased to know aught that was passing around me. There was reason to think, as I learned afterwards, that I was under religious conviction, and the delicacy with which they acted towards me on this account, prevented me from discovering anything said or thought respecting me. I came, therefore, to be left to the solitude which was at once my wish and my torment. It is not to be doubted, that had some discreet Christian contrived to fall in with me, and engage affectionately in conversation on religion, until he could have learned something respecting the peculiarity of my situation, I might have been taken by the hand, and with the light of the gospel, been conducted out of a despondency which to me was like the valley of the shadow of death, into a region illuminated with the brightness of heaven, and the smiles of God's favor. But I have reason to believe that I appeared to others so anxious to conceal my situation, and possibly betrayed such sensitiveness to every thing that bore allusion to it, that no one was willing to attempt an intrusion into my confidence. What makes me think that a balm might have been poured into my diseased feelings, that would have been attended with grateful relief, and not been rejected as offered by an impertinent interference, is, that after long continuance in this suffering state, some person in whom I had confidence, did take occasion from some expression incidentally thrown out on my part, to advert to the satisfactions of religion; and the manner in which it was done, made me grateful, as though I saw in him the friend of my heart.

The truth is, as the reader is well aware, that a morbid melancholy had settled upon me. It is of no consequence how futile and senseless was the cause. This will only show that the precariousness of our temporal happiness may spring, not from evils that are real and inevitable merely, but from sources which, if you will, exist in the imagination only, and are in their true merits equivalent to nothing. Religion is the proper and only effectual cure of all the ills that humanity "is heir to." Ignorance, misconceptions, the natural darkness of the soul, or a diseased action of the body upon the mind, may sink the unhappy subject into desperation; but in every case, could the gospel be brought to bear upon him, not with a perverted, but with its genuine influence, the remedy is infallible and complete. Its action in the instant it is felt, will be pronounced to be the very infusion into the wounded spirit which heals wherever it is felt, carrying along with it energy and joy that are like "life from the dead."

The reader will see that at a period of my life as happy as any which I had ever known, which had been of long continuance, and to which I suspected no interruption, it was broken as suddenly as a vessel of glass is dashed in pieces, not by the loss of property or friends, not by a fit of sickness, the necessary amputation of a limb, or the stopping up of one of my senses, but by a glancing thought of imagination only, converting a bosom into a scene of darkness and desolation, where all, till then had been light and cheerfulness. I sometimes struggled for deliverance, from an occasional supposition, that such might really be the nature of my affection. But in every effort, though resolutely made, I was fairly overpowered, and felt myself brought down irresistibly into the dust. I discovered upon a few occasions incidentally occurring, that being in company my thoughts were stolen away from the dejecting apprehensions that usually occupied them, and my spirits would mount unawares to the gaiety once familiar to them. But in less than an hour after returning into solitude, I found myself again prostrate under the same incumbent pressure, though I recollect that at the moment I manfully determined no more to yield to it. After a continuance of some two or three months in this wretched state, I came to a conclusion that to prosecute education any longer in circumstances so disqualifying and disheartening promised no valuable result, and that it was too much for me to continue to bear. The issue to which I arrived was, to obtain permission to leave the college, and should I live to study a profession, to apply myself to the study of medicine. The explanation was made to Dr. Witherspoon and Dr. Smith, and they listened to it apparently with regret. They spoke of the importance of completing an education whatever my profession might be. It terminated in a recommendation to visit my friends for two or three weeks; that possibly my health might be improved; and if it should be, by all means to return as soon as possible to my studies. They doubtless suspected the true cause of my difficulties, and their advice was fitted to the removal of them. To get home was but an afternoon's ride in the stage, and after being there a few days I discovered that the state of my feelings began sensibly to change. I had grown into the habit of daily prayer, and it was not long before my mother without my knowledge discovered it, to her great satisfaction. I staid out the three weeks, and so surprising was the recovery of my mental firmness and emancipation from the bondage which had so long bowed me to the earth, that I felt no difficulty in resolving to return and resume the studies to which I had once determined to bid adieu forever.

It may be asked, perhaps, in what light I considered the experience through which I passed in regard to its religious influence, and whether it was deemed by myself to be attended with true conviction of sin, or to terminate in a change of heart? To this I feel compelled to answer in the negative. My heart was too much in a state of bondage through the fear of death, to agree to the character of one renovated by the faith of the gospel. I never enjoyed any of the satisfactions of religion, springing from love to God, and confidence in his mercy, through Christ's atonement, as the means or the pledge of pardon and acceptance as an heir of life. Could I have experienced this, it would probably have dispersed the thick and dreary cloud that hovered around me, and would have darted sunshine through the soul. It was a spirit of depression and despondency, as if all hope were blighted, and I could look with no complacency upon the present or the future. I struggled for deliverance, but every effort was felt to be in vain. I engaged in prayer because I dreaded the final judgment of the Almighty, to which, in my apprehension, I might soon be called. Looking on this life as having no interests *for me*, and on death as all that intervened between the present and the irretrievable loss that was to follow, every resource was cut off to which I might look for some satisfaction to beam upon my mind, or replace its dejection with joy and courage. And that which makes me think the more that I had none of the true spirit of a child of God is, that in my wishes for relief, I thought but little of its nature, provided only I could effect an escape from the dreadful gloom which constituted my misery. The consequence was, that in a very short time after my return to cheerfulness and confidence, my thoughtlessness of God, of piety, and a future world, in too great a degree returned with them, until at length my mind became as worldly as ever.

It has been already mentioned that Dr. Witherspoon lived a mile from town. It was already a long time that he had retired from the daily and personal supervision of the college. He had become advanced in years, and after passing much of his life, not only in an active and efficient management of the institution, but in a participation of public affairs, and as a member of Congress in the Revolutionary War, he sought exemption from the daily cares of collegiate government, leaving its maintenance principally in the hands of Dr. Smith, who had married his daughter, and who held the vice-presidency. Mrs. Witherspoon, whom he had married in Scotland, died while I was a student, and some time afterwards it appeared that even at that late period he resolved upon another marriage. One morning, shortly after prayers, it was rumored among us that the Doctor had set out very early, in the old family carriage for Philadelphia. It was soon confirmed, to the surprise of all, for the matter had been conducted in brief time, and principally, if not entirely, by correspondence, with a lady of his acquaintance. He took breakfast that morning with Dr. Armstrong, in Trenton, twelve miles on the way. Dr. A. felt the subject to be of a delicate nature, and forebore all allusion to it, especially as Dr. Witherspoon said nothing respecting it himself. Dr. W. was but little in the habit of appearing in the style of that morning's equipment; probably it had been some years since the wheels of the ancient vehicle had rolled under him. To make out a competent number of animals for the draught, (less than four, it seems, would not do,) some were called into this higher service, from the more humble functions of the cart or the plough. It could not be expected, therefore, that they should appear in uniform, as if they had been originally selected for purposes such as that for which they were now arranged. As speedily after the dispatch of breakfast as might be, the visitor and the visited passed to the door, one for the continuance of his journey, the other to show honor to his guest, as well as gratitude for the privilege he had enjoyed. For truly Dr. Witherspoon's conversation could multiply many times the pleasure of a breakfast served up to a man in the best manner, by his own fireside, and in the most auspicious circumstances. As ill luck would have it, if that can properly be called luck which the circumstances rendered almost inevitable, the first thing that caught the eye of Dr. Armstrong, and in easy good nature prompted the tongue, was the disparity in size, color, and form that reigned luxuriantly among the quadrupeds. "Why, Doctor," was his remark in pleasantry, "you do not seem to be very well matched." It will not appear strange if to one upon the verge of being a bridegroom, at any age, though it might be sixty-two, which happened to be the Doctor's, the image of horses, absorbing as that might be which was furnished by his own, was not uppermost in his thought. And this might especially be expected, when the one to whom he looked to be the bride, was in all the bloom and fullness of two and twenty. That, therefore, befell which the two friends had most studiously, and till this very last moment, successfully eluded. The one spoke of horses, the other thought of matrimony; and the reply of the Doctor was, "I neither give advice, nor do I take any." This was said as he ascended into the vehicle, and both the coachman and his animals commenced their respective functions with an action commensurate with their energies.

A few days elapsed, and one morning it was whispered among the students that on the previous evening the Doctor had returned with his bride. This was at first offered in the shape of a surmise only. But such a subject could not be permitted to rest without more light than what the night had thrown upon it. It was soon ascertained to be a fact, and a few of us were forthwith deputed to solicit the intermission of business for a day at least, that we might all manifest our joy, and do honor to the occasion. We soon arrived near the Doctor's mansion, and while we were yet some distance from the door, he presented himself for our reception. We were not a little delighted to be greeted with a welcome beyond what we felt ourselves assured in anticipating. We were invited with a flow of feeling such as we had never observed in the Doctor, to enter, and then advancing to the side-board, to join with him in a glass of wine, which needed not to have been so well selected as it was, to prove to us highly palatable and cheering. Being commended to drink to the health of the bride, we answered by uniting that of the bridegroom also, with a respectful wish, and I am sure an ardent one too, flowing from the bottom of our hearts, for their happiness through many years to come. We informed him that we appeared on the part of the college to ask some release from ordinary business on an occasion so gratifying to us all, and that we might have opportunity of manifesting our joy. "Yes, by all means, if it is your wish," was the reply. "At such a time as this, we must admit a suspension of business for two days at least, if not three." In the length of time spoken of, a discovery was made of something beyond our most sanguine expectations. It was one, as may be supposed, in which we could see nothing to mar our satisfaction. We were delighted to the full, and though we could not press him to our bosoms, he found his way to our hearts. We took our leave with grateful expressions, and hastened back with the tidings to our fellow students.

At the close of the third day, a large piece of ordnance, a thirty-six pounder I think, which was a relict of the Revolutionary contest, had been brought up and placed before the college. At the first fire, as a signal, the whole front appeared illuminated as in an instant: at the second, in an hour or two afterwards, the light was as suddenly extinguished. This was the conclusion of the three days allowed us, falling little short in hilarity of feeling to our young bosoms, of that which had been excited in older minds six years before, when intelligence was received that definite articles of peace had been signed at the British court, recognizing the independence of these United States. I have related these incidents of a college life, because to some they may be amusing, who have been themselves familiar with it: to others who have not, they will serve as specimens of the manner in which students live, or may be affected in their peculiar circumstances.

It is a question which may easily occur, whether the youth is happier who passes his early years in a University, or he who is reared to an occupation which through the same period calls him to bodily labor. The inquiry may be extended to the whole of life. It may be asked whether any one has a greater prospect of enjoyment in a life of diligent mental or corporeal occupation. As to indolence or unfaithfulness in the prosecution of either, they are not to be brought into view, both because they are unworthy of our consideration, and if mixed with the subject, must make it wholly indefinite. It is certainly very common with students to pant after the privileges of a rural life; and perhaps it is no less so for the son of the farmer, who is constrained to daily toil, as every one ought to be who is to follow that profession, to feel convinced that the opportunities of a liberal education would crown his utmost wishes. It is probable that the unhappiness of each is chiefly due, not to the nature of his business, but to the indulgence of an unsettled mind, and of complaint against the renewed exertion and confinement that return upon him in uninterrupted continuance. Each of them knows and feels his own difficulties and discontents, and it is through these that his conclusion is drawn unfavorably to his own employment. Each looks at the occupation of the other through imagination only. This selects the objects and colors of the picture, and he longs for the pleasures on which his eye is directed, without having forced upon his feelings the toils and solicitudes which experience would teach him to be inseparable from them. An actual subjection to these would soon convince him that nothing was gained by the exchange, were he allowed to make it. The true secret of human happiness, so far as profession is concerned, is probably to be seen, not so much in the employment, as in that discipline over ourselves which by directing our efforts upon the greatest efficacy and skill in the performance of every thing we would do, becomes interested in the result, and in the true and efficient means of its attainment. Let not the farmer or the mechanic, nor let their sons look with envy upon the privileges of the student. Placed in his situation, subjected to his confinement, and to the same rigorous exaction upon his mental faculties in the daily task, he would probably soon sigh for exemption from them, that he might be replaced in the condition which he had deserted with fond and disappointed calculations. A student sometimes returns home from the academy or the college, repining or clamoring with discontent, and soliciting as a privilege to be employed in some manual or bodily exertion, rather than continue under the pressure and restriction of a college life. He is perhaps gratified by his parent. A short trial convinces him of his misapprehensions, and he eagerly compromises for a return to that from which his feelings had so strongly revolted. This furnishes no evidence in behalf of collegiate felicity, any more than that the blistering of the hands, or the soreness of the muscles by the labor of the first days, would prove that the same effects and the sufferings from them are to be borne continually, should he addict himself to labor through the whole of life. Before we can be enured to any species of industry, some uneasy, if not painful effects, must be experienced. A mind unalterably fixed upon its purpose will find these to be trifles. Once seasoned to its occupation, it is better capable of determining the satisfactions it is to enjoy in the choice which it has made. Nor will it then do justice to its own election, if doubt and vacillation be not perfectly excluded. In proportion as these are permitted to agitate the breast, they will prove elements of dissolution to our happiness. All envy at the imagined superior advantages of others, all repugnance and fretfulness at the obstacles or inconveniences that meet us as we advance, are an unreasonable quarrel with the laws of nature, and the determinations of Providence; and if that be our temper, every situation and every profession will harrass us with their occurrence in sufficient numbers to make us dissatisfied with our lot. One who often counts the hours that are passing, or which are yet to come before a release from his business, is likely to find it too long for his wishes. Another who looks to the objects he is bent on accomplishing, will be apt to think it too short, and instead of abridging the day, he longs to extend it. The one who improves his time with diligence, receiving it as it is meted out to him, in the prosecution of his settled purpose, admitting no wavering uncertainties to weaken or tease him with discontents furnishes a third description of character; and which of them is likely to exceed in happiness, cannot be difficult of determination. Let not the student, or the professional man, envy the mechanic, or the farmer. It implies that he wants self-discipline, and if he continue long unhappy, the fault is in himself and not in his circumstances. Nor let the person whose business calls him to muscular action, imagine that in literary, or professional life, he would be more highly favored. It is to this very indulgence of an uncertain mind that he owes all his miseries. But who can be happy without reference to God? How shall any man, young or old, rationally hope to be blest, if his plans be all chosen and pressed forward without the admission of the principle that He rules and must be consulted in all our affairs? In our diligence, our danger is that we shall rest in our own efficacy, and the sufficiency of the world. If this be our spirit, it is essentially an error, nor is it one of minor consequence, which may take place, and yet we make our way with disadvantages only. It is an error more fatal to our plans and efforts, at least to our happiness, than any other can be. This would appear to carry with it the evidence of a first truth, an indisputable axiom, to the judgment of the most enlightened mind, as well as the humblest christian. The man who admits this, not merely as a general principle when he happens to come to it, but habitually and practically, in his meditations and the execution of his plans, will find himself carried forward by consistency to a complete acknowledgement of the gospel.

After a continuance of four years and a half from the time of my joining the senior class in the grammar-school, we were graduated in 1791, my age being then eighteen years and a half. The delight I felt on that occasion must have been excited by a disenthralment from the confining rules and the ever-returning responsibilities of a college life, rather than by any prospect of circumstances more exuberant in happiness. My education was all that I could look to; my fortune was to be made, and not one definite object was before me to give direction to my movements. The gay feelings that spread through my bosom were overcast by a sombrous aspect, diffusing through them a pensiveness that sometimes almost oppressed me. I had always been successful in my studies, and this was an encouragement. But my views were altogether indefinite; the world was before me, and I knew not how I was to get hold of it, that I might bring any ability I might possess into action, gain advantages, and then make them avail for the acquisition of more. I had not even decided the profession I was to follow, and of course could not look any where for this species of preparation. I was young, however; my spirits were cheerful. One thought in which I indulged was, that I had time to spare before coming of age, and that I might afford to pass some of it in amusement, in reprisal for the long confinement from which I was now emancipated. This was an unhappy mistake, for I acted so much upon it, that the improvement of a year or two was lost; which time, had it been faithfully applied in a course of valuable studies, would have added largely to my attainments. I went to reside with my mother and brother, who were now at Black River, near Flanders, where he lived as a farmer upon the land once my grandmother's, and which she had bequeathed to him at her death.

Some months passed away in idleness, or little better. I grew weary of it, but knew not what to do. I was among farmers, and yet wholly unqualified to participate in their interests or occupations. I found that capital without a market was of no value. They looked upon me as a scholar, but they had no use for scholarship, and I was in danger of falling into disesteem, if not contempt, from the inefficacy of all that I possessed for any profit to them or to myself.

At length it was suggested by some of them, that a few boys in the village and neighborhood wanted instruction in the languages. It was proposed that I should teach them; and so weary was I of doing nothing, that I took refuge in the employment, though I thought it an humble business. It was an easy business to me, and I took pleasure in looking again at the beauties of Virgil, and unfolding them to my scholars. I continued some months to do this, but it was felt to be a matter of small moment in comparison with the larger and higher objects of imagination. It was still a difficulty to know how to get at them. They rose up in numerous and picturesque forms, but in my youthful inexperience and inability to address myself to men, to make propositions or present inducements to them, it seemed that it was all fancy only, which I began at last to think was never to be realized.

Whatever else may enter into the purposes of the young, love is certain to constitute a part. Some of our neighbors, as must always happen, made a figure in property and consequence above others. Next door but one to ours, was a family of this description. A young lady was of its number, who I found began to fasten upon me in a manner so pleasing, that I had no disposition to displace the thought of her by any reflections which might be at variance with it as an inmate of my bosom. My morning walks soon came to be decidedly more frequent by her house, than in the opposite direction. If she happened to be visible, which was not unfrequently the case, as northern families in the country are apt to be in the habit of bestirring themselves early, my eye would steal glances towards her, which would serve to make the time till I returned home, pass with more vivid enjoyment of the fresh air, the scenery around, the alacrity of healthful sensation, and the enchanting tints diffused by fancy over the fields, and every subject of my thoughts. As yet our intercourse had been but infrequent. We were both young, and could scarcely venture to think of a matter involving such serious consequences as matrimony. It was to our early minds too distant to be realized. Such at least I deemed to be the state of her sentiments, from her manner, so far as I had observed it. She was willingly communicative, but rather pensive than gay. Her father had been educated for the ministry, but being of a slender constitution, and somewhat apprehensive of pectoral weakness, he had made choice of a farmer's life, that he might be called into activity, augment bodily strength, and prevent that reaction of the mind which might overpower it. Her mother was an excellent woman, but fell much short of her husband in sprightliness and intelligence.

At length as my walks would recur, for they were agreeable, it seemed observable that I was seldom, if ever, disappointed in seeing her; and when she appeared, it was not in a passing manner only, as at first, but when I came into view her movement lingered, her eye became directed upon mine, which, in spite of a repressive feeling of modesty to which I was exceedingly subject, was sure to be turned upon her, and we would almost stop under the influence that certainly fascinated me, and to which I could not but flatter myself she was not wholly insensible. If the wings of Mercury had been put upon my feet, I could not have felt lighter after observations like these. My heart began to run upon this object with renewed interest through the day. And whenever the thought of Miss O—— returned, the probability that if I should seek a more intimate acquaintance, the proffer would not be declined, excited in my young bosom trembling emotions, to be set down under the head of enjoyment; for time which had before dragged heavily, now glided along with a pleasing smoothness, and my uneasiness at the idea that I was making no headway towards the prospects to which I looked with indefinite contemplation, but determined purpose, ceased to torment me. My walks were still renewed, as I did not fail to be gratified with the appearance of her who was now their principal motive, I loitered as I drew near, and when the bow and the good morning were offered with a smile of interest and complacency, they were returned with expression and manner which I thought I could not misunderstand. I stood still and entered into conversation. The soft and pleasant tones of her voice, with her willingness to listen and reply, without any appearance of a disposition to terminate the interview, gave delightful intimations that something of the same sentiment was alive in her bosom, which was thrilling in mine.

After this our acquaintance grew more intimate. I visited the family sometimes, and my reception implied that there was no unwillingness that my visits should be continued. But to what purpose was all this? was an inquiry which began to press much upon me, and to occupy my thoughts as though I was engaged in an inconsistency with which I could not be satisfied. I had never given up the idea that my destiny was to be marked out, not in the place where I then was, but somewhere at large, in some other sphere, for the one in which I then moved was felt to be of dimensions too diminutive to satisfy me. These considerations, though thrust out of sight by the force of my first youthful experience of a passion that reigns in the bosoms of all, began to weigh heavily upon me, whenever an approximation to the final issue compelled me to look upon it as but a few steps before me. I pretend not to say whether, if the plan of a matrimonial connection with this young lady whose charms had given me more knowledge of what it was to love than I had before acquired, had been urged to a determination, it would or would not have been successful. It was a question which in the existing circumstances, I felt too appalling to bring to a crisis. Had it been pressed to a successful conclusion, it would have undoubtedly furnished another instance of Providential disposition, by which the whole course of my life would have been permanently directed by a turn, as upon the minutest pivot, into a channel wholly different from that in which it has flowed. To myself alone it can be supposed a matter of any interest. But when every other person directs his eye upon similar instances in his own history, in which circumstances the most trivial have given a shape to the whole of his subsequent condition in the world, the reflection becomes obvious and impressive, by what small events Providence guides the destinies of our existence.

While in this situation which seemed tending to a crisis, and not long after its last peculiarities which had been so delicately interesting to me had occurred, I received notice, I scarcely remember how, that my services as an assistant teacher would be acceptable in Elizabethtown, in the lower part of the State. No hesitation was felt in accepting the offer. I left Black River forever, my studies were renewed, and the opportunities of a polished community, and literary society were relished more exquisitely after the tedious and dismal sequestration I had suffered. My companionship, and the privileges of living under a ministry and in a congregation where religion was highly estimated, and its impressions were often deeply felt, proved the means of turning my thoughts and affections anew and with more intensity on that subject. The result was such that the question of a profession, which had never yet been decided, terminated in a conclusion, if God would sanction it with his grace, that I would commence a course of studies for the sacred ministry. With much diffidence and apprehension, I entered on the prosecution of these subjects under the direction of the Rev. David Austin, then pastor of the Presbyterian congregation in the place. A relative of his by the name of Sherman, was my companion in study. My obligations both to the uncle and the nephew, for their personal kindness and encouragement, have ever been remembered with the deepest and most affectionate gratitude. Poor Sherman, as himself told me some years afterwards, in a letter, renounced Orthodoxy and espoused Socinianism. Other events afterwards befell, distressing and mortifying in their nature, which were successively heard of by me with surprise and regret. They must have been humiliating to him, but it is useless to repeat them here. They imply nothing, however, that will affect his moral character, except it were true, as I was told, that he became, at least in some degree, intemperate.

Some months after commencing the study of Divinity, it was proposed to me to undertake the instruction of an academy at Springfield. To obtain funds, I entered into negotiation upon the subject. The gentlemen who spoke of it, appeared to me at first rather cool and reserved for my feelings, for their manner implied some apprehension respecting the result. I felt and manifested more independence than was consistent with my circumstances, for it was really a matter of some consequence to me to engage in the business. While we were conversing on preliminaries, and were on the point of reaching a conclusion, a letter came from Dr. Smith, of Princeton, proposing that I should become a tutor in the college. As soon as these gentlemen were aware of this, they manifested no small surprise and agitation, and their urgency grew continually, until while I persevered in my conclusion to accept of the tutorship, I was in danger of being charged with improperly disappointing them, as though a contract had been already made. On this, however, they could by no means insist. I asked them whether as friends, they would advise me to accept of their offer in preference to my prospects at Princeton. They candidly replied that they could not, and so we parted upon sufficiently good terms.

At the college I instantly began to feel the vast difference between the privileges of a student in a place where science and literature were the professional occupation of all around me, and abroad in the world, where the prosecution of these objects not only was unsupported by a community of feelings and interests, except perhaps with one or two, but seclusion from much intercourse was indispensably necessary to any tolerable success. In the midst of professors, and scholars, and libraries, bent upon as great attainments as I could compass, having a taste for learning and intent on qualifying myself liberally for a profession, I was happy in expatiating upon classic ground, and desired nothing so much as the very privileges I enjoyed of traversing the volumes which it was my duty to take as my guides to the ulterior purposes before me. Nothing troubled me so much as an interruption of my studies. This had been much the case through the whole course of my education, and as my disposition was in general kindly towards others, I never could well understand how numbers of young men could be prompted as they evidently were, not only to lavish as much time as possible in idleness, but to interpose obstructions with almost a spirit of malignity and persecution, in the way of others who were studious of abstraction and improvement. It is evident, however, that where there is no community of sentiment among men, they are not satisfied with neutrality or indifference toward one another, but grow into opposition and even mutual hatred. To prevent this, self-discipline is more or less necessary. Its cultivation and establishment through society is one evidence of superior civilization. But the spirit of forbearance can never be fully comprehended, but by the exposition of the gospel to the mind and the heart, not in their ordinary natural state, but as they are made capable of the proper feelings of this virtue, by the Spirit of Him who revealed and illustrated it in the scriptures. And if forbearance, which is but a negative virtue, cannot be known and felt without such a reformation, much less can the spirit of that positive celestial charity be supposed producible by us, which binds all in the creation that are under its influence, to the throne of God and to one another in ties, which by his own formation, are the certain and only pledge at once of individual and universal happiness.

The same variance in taste, sentiment, and interest is exhibited in the little society of a college, as agitates the world at large, through its communities and governments. There is no condition, indeed, in which we may not learn human nature, and find it the very same in one as in another. In every one will be enough of the evil passions and obliquities to sicken or wound us with their offensive forms, and thanks be to Him who preserves and governs this world as a probationary state in mercy, there is a mixture of better characters and qualities, sufficient not merely to reconcile us to the evil, but to create attachments even in the best of men, by which they cling to their objects as with a dying grasp.

While residing at Princeton this third and last time, an incident occurred once more of a nature to impress upon me awfully the perfect uncertainty of life, while we are in the height of its enjoyments, in the vigor of youth, and when the peril is unsuspected the moment before we are involved in it. A young man fully grown, by the name of Simpson, was a student of the college. It happened that some intimacy grew between us, as might easily be, as I occupied a room in the college building. In the warm season of the year, we agreed to take an early walk to the usual place of bathing, because the air would be fresh, and we should be without other company. Simpson, though of full size and age, could swim but little; scarcely with skill and confidence enough to venture into deep water. It was different with me, and while he was practising in shallow places, the freedom and repitition of my passages over the deeper parts, there was reason to think became a temptation to him. In setting off from where he was to pass up the stream, which could not be done without swimming further than he had ever before attempted, I called out to him with a cheering voice, and without thinking whether he would make the trial or not, to follow on. I arrived at the shallow water above, and on turning round was surprised to see him arrived at the middle of the deepest part. He seemed to be doing very well, and I told him so for his encouragement. Almost instantly afterwards I saw him place himself deliberately in an erect attitude, and descend as we generally do, to try the depth of the water. His appearance was so much that of self-possession, that it seemed handsomely done; but when he rose, as a little afterwards he did, his person shooting almost half above the surface, and the water projecting a full stream from his mouth, a sudden horror seized me; I saw that he had given out at the time when he went down; in his confusion, he had hoped the depth might not be too great for him; it was, however, far over his head, and, if he had held his breath at all, he had instantly ceased to do so, Without assistance, he must inevitably drown, perhaps before I could get to him to afford it, even if I were able. I was aware of the convulsive struggles of a drowning man, and had often heard how dangerous. I was small and light; he was larger than the ordinary size in bone and muscle, and had the appearance of unusual strength. The moment I saw him in that desperate situation a sudden compunction flashed through me for having probably been the occasion of his losing his life, when I so rashly spoke to him to follow from the starting place; and, beside this, I could not indulge for a moment the thought of seeing him drown without an effort to save him. All these considerations passed through my mind in far less than the time necessary to their utterance, for we think with almost incredible rapidity in such extreme emergencies. In fact, he had no sooner disappeared again, after rising out of the water, than I was on the way, whatever was to be the consequence.

In passing to the spot where he was struggling with death, I observed that he still continued to project himself above the water from the bottom, as often as he sunk. My plan for getting him out was, to avoid his grasp by going up behind him, in such a manner that by reaching out my right hand in front and taking hold of his left arm near the shoulder, I might exert upon him, steadily, as much force as was necessary to support his head above water, and so push him forward to the shore, depending on the other arm and my feet for swimming. This method was thought of on the way, for when I set out I really had not considered how the object was to be accomplished. It was, I believe, the third time of his appearing above the water, when I was so near him as to arrive where he was, against the next time, and place myself for taking hold of him, should he come up once more. While he was in view this third time, I called out to him with a voice exerted to the utmost, "To let me alone, and I would get him out." I certainly did not reflect in the pressure of the moment, that he might as well have been expected to hear me and follow my directions, as if he had been in the remotest extremity of the globe. He arose once more, and finding myself precisely in the position I wished, I attempted to grasp his arm, but as I might have anticipated, it was too large for one so much smaller as I was than himself, especially at that part, and beside this the smoothness occasioned by the water, and the convulsive violence of his motions, convinced me at once that my scheme was utterly hopeless. He went down once more, and I was filled with horror in the despair of saving him. The next moment, however, I felt his fingers grappling at my legs, with such an indication in the manner as shocked me with the conviction that if he succeeded in laying hold on me, which had now evidently become his object, we must both drown together. In an instant I was in the utmost stretch of exertion to escape from him. Still his hands now and then continued to be felt, and always with a terrifying violence. I was convinced that I had swam far enough to be out of his way, and could not imagine how it could be that when I was persuading myself that I must be safe, his contact filled me with fresh alarm. I began to think that it would be impossible to elude him. My efforts, however, were of course continued, though I knew nothing of the direction in which they were made, until my breast struck upon the shore. I was surprised when this occurred, that it should have been so completely invisible to me. No sooner had it happened than turning round, I saw Simpson standing erect upon his feet, within four feet of me, his eyes closed, and the water shooting out of his mouth in a copious and continued stream. The relief felt when my own safety was ensured was as great as it was sudden, but how exquisite was the joy when I saw that he too was secure. While I had been making my way to the best of my ability at the surface of the water, he had been instinctively pursuing hard after me, though buried under it, and had felt the bottom in the same moment that I had touched the shore. He had been long struggling in the arms of death, but to my astonishment it soon appeared that I was much more exhausted than he. In walking half the mile we had to go to the college, my strength was wholly gone, and sinking upon the ground, I called upon him to give me time to rest. He showed no extreme debility, but seemed able to walk the whole distance without any such distress. My system certainly had no claims to the strength of his, but although while in the water, before missing my aim at his arm, I had retained perfect self-possession; from the moment I felt his clutch, it must have been a perfect panic with me, and my powers were overdone by the intensity of action that followed. The consequent langor, however, was not of long continuance. Rest, and the first meal produced no small repairs, and the pleasure felt for the safety of us both, probably hastened the system to its usual activity, so that by the next day the effects were no more perceptible.

I shall not think it worth while to note many incidents of my second continuance at Princeton, except that I was called to act as tutor in the college, and one other.

In the tutorship my time was principally occupied in giving critical perfection, as far as possible, to my knowledge of the classical authors which it was my business to teach. This was at once my duty and my delight. It may be supposed, of course, that my qualifications to instruct were not questioned. But the part of a tutor's office which consists in government, is by no means certain to run parallel with knowledge and the ability to communicate it. This was the occasion of much solicitude;

and of more trial to my feelings than I should have consented to bear, had it not been that advantages of improvement of a practical nature recommended it, and that the necessity of funds imposed it upon me. My feelings were always delicate and sensitive, and this put it easily into the power of those to whom the thought of being under authority was uppermost as ungrateful in their situation, to take revenge upon the unfortunate being whose indispensable duty it was to enforce the rules of the college. No provocation was necessary to call into action a spirit of mischief, tumult, and attack. No plea of necessity for quiet to the success of study, or for decorum and respect for the enjoyment of privileges and credit in society, was of sufficient avail to repress disorderly conduct, or prevent it from growing into outrage if it was not met and resisted. He, then, who exercises authority, especially over the young, may expect to be unreasonably assailed by some at least, whose study it will be, and who will therefore be far more successful than in prosecuting their education, to puncture his feelings, and to inflict torture upon them in an exquisite degree. The true and only remedy for such evils is forbearance, cordial solicitude for the real welfare of the young whose tuition is entrusted to us, and unremitting fidelity to the obligations binding us to the institution that looks to us for a conscientious discharge of the office it has devolved upon us, and for which we have made ourselves responsible. The instructor in whose bosom these motives are habitually alive, may, and will be, thoughtlessly or rudely assailed by the unfeeling, the discontented, and the unreasonable; but his motives and proper character will be irresistibly felt, and in the hour of trial he will be sustained against all the efforts of obloquy and opposition. It is difficult, if not impossible, for a young man acting in a tutorship to know at all times the estimation that attends him in his personal or official character. Incidents will occur to make him feel himself disparaged and depressed. The wounds which appear intentionally inflicted upon him, are apt to be felt much more deeply than accords to the real merits of the case, and if the officer be not mercifully inclined, he may easily exceed in the infliction of punishment. The conviction of the offender in his own mind, and his reclamation from his fault, are certainly the first objects of a teacher, and scarcely to be relinquished, until all the efforts of reason and affectionate solicitude have failed, and the stubbornness and invincible adherence to a bad cause, after time for reflec- tion, have decided his case to be hopeless. The student who yields in such a struggle, furnishes greater assurance against future disorder or mis- conduct, than can be gained by a treatment that aims to deter by severity; and if he persist, the penalty which becomes necessary, will ensure all the efficacy which it is the proper object of exemplary discipline to secure. He who seeks to win the heart upon correct principles, will with difficulty be resisted.   If he even be met in return with rudeness and insolence, let him not despair, for these if rightly received, furnish fresh pledges of final success.

In the beginning of September, 1796, I set out upon my journey to North Carolina.   Mr. Charles Harris of that State had been acquainted with me while he was a student of Nassau Hall.   It was but a year that he was at Princeton, for he entered the Senior Class on his admission into the college.   So little had been our personal intercourse with one another, that I afterward scarcely remembered that I had ever seen him.   This was about the year 1791.   In 1796, the University of North Carolina had commenced its business, and Mr. Harris was acting as Professor of Mathe- matics.   Having determined to make the law his profession, he accepted the professorship for a short time only, and at the close of the year he was to relinquish his place in the college.   He had understood that I was in the tutorship at Princeton, and sent me a letter to know whether I would consent to be appointed his successor.   I was as incompetent as a child to determine the answer I ought to give.   I could do nothing but refer the question to others whom I supposed better judges, and whom I had reason to consider as my best and sincerest friends.   The opinion of most, if not all, was, that I ought to accept the offer if it should be made. As to myself, it was flattering to my feelings, and presented a prospect of respectable and permanent income.   I had but little practical knowledge of men, but felt quite convinced that if I was qualified to engage at once in any species of business, it was in teaching rather than any thing else. If my acquaintance with the world, even where I had grown up into it, was but small, of that part of it into which I was going, it might be liter- ally said that I knew nothing.   I might have had an idea that some dif- ference was to be seen in the state of society, and in the manners and customs of the people; but in what the peculiarities specifically consisted, I certainly had no conception.   It was concluded that it was best to travel by private conveyance, and after bidding an adieu, more trying to my feel- ings than I had supposed it was to be, I found myself with horse and gig on the road to Philadelphia.   I stopped at Dr. Armstrong's, in Trenton, to receive from him letters of introduction to gentlemen of Hillsborough, in North Carolina, where he had resided some time with the American army as chaplain during the Revolutionary War.   Coming to Philadel- phia on a Saturday, I was invited to preach the next day in Dr. Green's pulpit in Arch street.   On Monday morning, one or two elderly gentle- men, who appeared incidentally to call, began to say that they had under- stood I was on a journey to another part of the country, but they had started the question whether it might not be possible and expedient to stop me where I was.   They alluded to a vacant pulpit, which it seems, some suggestion had been made, that I might be invited to occupy as pastor. To this Dr. Green suddenly, and in a manner somewhat more decisive than was agreeable to me at the moment, remarked that the matter he believed to be totally decided : that I was on my way to Carolina, and that to Carolina he understood I was certainly to go. It would be to no purpose, therefore, to speak of plans which might be at variance with this. My disposition was exceedingly pliant at that age; I had been accustomed to look to others for determination more than to myself; the suggestion had struck suddenly upon my ear; my mind, it was true, had felt itself conclusively settled as to its object, and although there was an instantaneous and involuntary start of revolt in my bosom at the promptness with which Dr. Green undertook to pronounce for me, the matter passed away without any thing farther said, and the next day I again found myself on the road. The gentlemen who had entered Dr. Green's house, and commenced with the remark respecting the object of my journey, which they had learned, I knew not how, undoubtedly were about to propose that I should remain some little time in the city, to give further opportunity to some vacant congregation to which they probably belonged as elders, to form an opinion of me as a minister, and determine whether they might not give me a call. On this I have sometimes ruminated, as to the effects it might have produced upon the whole aspect of my life, had their proposition been listened to, and followed by a relinquishment of my prospects in the South, for a pulpit and a congregation in the city. It has impressed upon me anew, how surprisingly we are in the hands of God's providential interposition.

Should we place an elastic ball upon an immense plain, and imagine a motion given to it which would continue through the distance of 70 miles, and that it was subject, every now and then, to be acted on by impulses from other balls coming into contact in all various directions, sometimes laterally, sometimes obliquely in the direction of its motion, and then contrary to its direction, sometimes in the same line against, at other times in exact concurrence with its course, now with great efficacy, then with an action scarcely discernible, it would be a question of no easy solution, where such a rolling body was likely to be found at any period of its motion, how far it would have proceeded, or in what line it would be advancing. It would have set out with an impetus originally imparted to it, and which is afterwards its own, it ever continues with an impetus forward, and these have a share of influence in determining both its distance and its course, but it is only a portion of influence which it exerts. How much is ever depending upon other influences and impacts which in continual succession are meeting it on every side, and whose arrival both in time and place is wholly from without and independent of itself. Will not this serve as an analogous illustration of the life of a being setting out in the world, and advancing through it under the controlling power of an overruling Providence? Let it not be imagined that I would confound the distinction between moral and physical motives, or consider them the same in their nature. Were this true, all responsibility would be taken away, and fatality be alike applicable to the material and spiritual world. Moral action is wholly diverse in its very nature, from material action, and it is in this difference that we forever continue accountable for every choice we make, and every deed we perform. In this very circumstance we see the wonderful and unsearchable wisdom of God. We might have been made acquainted with one species of agency only, the physical: and then every result, and our whole progress through existence, would have been with no more accountableness on our part, than the ball would be answerable for its position or direction at any particular moment. But this it seems is not the only way which God can devise for the influences of Providence. He can connect with his government over his creatures, a responsibility as complete on their part, as though any exertion of power by himself were wholly excluded. Who shall deny this wisdom and this ability to God? All the issues of our lives are the result, not of physical necessity, but of moral certainty, so connected in us with freedom of choice, and felt with a conviction so complete, that when God judges us, every mouth shall be stopped, for we shall know that our [destiny as to happiness or misery, has been of our own framing. We cannot choose our own circumstances externally, but while we are standing in them, we can choose or retain our principles. It is by these that a character is imparted to us in the eye of our Heavenly Father, and it is with these that he connects our happiness or misery by inviolable conditions.

NOTE.

[The following NOTE was written by a relative and pupil of Dr. CALDWELL, who, it seems, intended to prepare a Biography of Dr. C. to accompany the Autobiography. From some cause he failed to execute that intention, and the preface to his biography is here inserted as it gives the motives which probably actuated the writer in penning the Autobiography.]

When a man dies who has filled a considerable space in the public eye, there seems to be a natural and just curiosity to know something of his private history, his parentage, his education, the events of Providence and the personal exertions by which he at length rose to merited distinction. This public interest in the history of a man who has been snatched by death from the stage of the world where he was acting a conspicuous part may be turned to valuable account. The memory of such an individual, who was of late the object of love and veneration, may be made a vehicle of much valuable instruction which would never have obtained access to the mind, if offered in a didactic form, unembodied with the narrative It is fortunate when the subject of the memoir, himself, has left us authentic materials for the history of the earlier and more obscure part of his life. The development of all that secret portion of a man's history which passes within his own bosom, the geography, if we may be allowed the figure, of that *terra incognita* which, though rich in veins of gold, must have remained always unknown, but for these personal disclosures, has often been found interesting enough to make amends for the absence of incidents and adventures, and has rendered Confessions and Autobiographies the most attractive of all publications. Such an advantage the writer of the present memoir enjoys, having found among the papers of his deceased relative two small manuscript volumes, containing an account of his life till the year 1796 when he set out for the State of North Carolina, at the invitation of the Trustees of the University to become Professor of Mathematics of that institution. This memoir of himself it has been thought best to introduce in the form in which it was found. It is supposed that the compiler of this volume will perform his task in a manner more gratifying to others who will take an interest in perusing it, if even a considerable portion of it should be occupied with personal narrative and private reflections rather than with sermons—a kind of composition with which, and that too of first-rate excellence, the world is already so full that there seems to be little use in increasing the stock All, I presume, which his friends and the public of North Carolina would desire besides the personal and official history, is a specimen of a few sermons, which together with that may furnish their libraries with a memento of the man who was thought so great a benefactor to this State and who is endeared to so many, as the preceptor and guide of their youth.

From several passages in the narrative it would appear not to have been intended for the public eye, but only designed for the perusal of his circle of friends and to furnish authentic materials in case any future account of him should be called for. The reader will, therefore, make requisite allowance for any want of care in the composition which he may discover. The complaint, however, will probably be of the opposite fault: too great formality and precision of expression, which it must be confessed characterized his style in a considerable degree, and of which he could not quite divest himself even in relating the familiar transactions of his private life. But although the reader will probably remark occasionally an involved and circuitous construction of his sentences, yet he will perhaps admit that oftentimes the thought is given forth with more strength from these tortuous involutions, as the stone from the sling, deriving impetus from its numerous gyrations.

BIOGRAPHY.[*]

A very brief notice of the early circumstances of the University of North Carolina, may not be misplaced or deemed impertinent here, as Dr. Caldwell's connection with it began in its infancy. The act of Corporation was past in 1789; but little efficient aid was given by the Legislature of the State towards the accomplishment of the undertaking. Grants of escheated property and of certain monies due to the State, and subsequently, of all confiscated property, were made; but of this latter source of revenue, the Trustees were soon afterwards divested, and the others were never very productive, except in Western Lands, the value of which remained for a long time little more than nominal, though at this day constituting a splendid endowment. Private munificence compensated the tardiness of the public benefactions. Gov. Benjamin Smith made a donation of twenty thousand acres of land; Major Charles Girard bequeathed thirteen thousand acres, and numerous contributions in money were made throughout the State, which enabled the Trustees to commence the buildings necessary for the accommodation of the students. But all these resources together were not commensurate with the magnitude of the enterprize; and the College struggled through a very feeble infancy for several years, until a development of its resources and the zeal and energy of its friends, brought it to a condition of more maturity and stability. The labors and constantly increasing reputation of Dr. Caldwell, were instrumental, in no small degree, in effecting this result; and he was permitted to live to see our Institution rising from the humble condition of a mere Grammer School, progressively through all the successive gradations of usefulness and respectability, to the high and honorable station which it occupied at his death among the Universities of the land. May we be pardoned for adverting here to one article in the Act of Incorporation, which seems to have been nugatory, from the limitation as to the time annexed to it, but the purpose of which might still be partly carried

---

*This Biographical Sketch of Dr. Caldwell is des'gned to illustrate the life of that great and good man after he became connected with the University of North Carolina in 1796. His early life is modestly narrated in the preceding pages by his own hand. We have not been able to procure a more copious narrative, therefore we have taken the liberty of re-publishing, with verbal and other modifications, the last part of the admirable "Oration on the Life and Character of Rev. Joseph Caldwell, D. D., L. L. D., delivered in 1835, by Professor Walker Anderson."

into effect in perfect consistency with its original design. It was enacted that six of the Halls, attached to the College precincts, should bear the names of the six individuals who, within four years, should be the largest contributors to the funds of the institution. It is probable, that with the exception of Gov. Smith's, there were not within that period any benefactions of such an amount as to warrant the Trustees in giving effect to this provisional act of gratitude; but the magnitude of one subsequent benefaction, at least, may well redeem it from the penalty annexed to its tardiness. Of the eight buildings constituting our present accommodations, one does honor to the name of one contributor, and the Chapel serves as a monument to the memory of another. The others are yet unappropriated; and, as we shall presently see, we are indebted for the largest of them, to funds accumulated from individual donations by the active exertions and persevering industry of Dr. Caldwell. He has been our most munificent benefactor, and to him should be awarded the highest meed of honor. Nor should the labors in our behalf of the lamented Mitchell go unremembered, when we come to christen our new edifices.

The business of Education in the University of North Carolina was commenced in the early part of the year 1795; Mr. Hinton James of Wilmington, the first Student, having arrived here on the 12th day of February of that year. The first Instructor was the Rev. David Kerr, a Graduate of Trinity College, Dublin, assisted by Mr. —— Holmes, in the Preparatory Department. Very shortly afterwards, the Professorship of Mathematics was filled by the appointment of Mr. Charles Harris, of Iredell county, and a Graduate of the College of New Jersey. It was not the intention of Mr. Harris to engage permanently in the business of Instruction, his views being directed to the Profession of the Law; and when he accepted the Professorship, it was with the understanding that he was to relinquish it at the expiration of one year. Mr. Harris, while at Princeton, had formed an acquaintance with Dr. Caldwell, but their personal intercourse was so slight, that the latter scarcely remembered that he had ever seen him. His recommendation of Dr. Caldwell, therefore, as his successor, is a proof of the high estimation in which the latter was held by all who had an opportunity of knowing him, and is a forcible illustration of the influence which undeviating rectitude and close attention to the duties of their station exercise over the future destinies of the young.

To the penetration of Mr. Harris, and his agency in filling the Professorship vacated by himself, with so competent a successor, North Carolinians owe an eternal debt of gratitude. The letter to Dr. Caldwell, enquiring whether he would accept the Professorship of Mathematics, reached him, as we learn in his autobiography, while engaged in the discharge of his Tutorship at Princeton, and employing such a portion of his time as could be spared from his more immediate business, in fitting himself for the ministerial office. The invitation being unsolicited, was unexpected, and found him wholly unprepared with an answer. The question was referred to his friends, who were supposed by him to be better judges than himself. They advised him to accept the offer; and, as it was flattering to his own feelings, and presented a prospect of a respectable and permanent income, he yielded to their advice, and accordingly signified to Mr. Harris his determination to accept the Professorship, if it should be offered him by the Trustees of the College. The appointment was made by an unanimous vote of the Board, and Dr. Caldwell, after being admitted to the ministry in the Presbyterian Church, left Princeton in the beginning of September 1796, for his journey to the South. While passing through Philadelphia, he was invited to preach in the pulpit of Dr. Ashbel Green, and made so favorable an impression, that inducements were held out to him to remain in the city, with a view of taking charge of a congregation there. By the advice of Dr. Green, he at once rejected the proposal and pursued his way to North Carolina. At the time that Dr. Caldwell became connected with the University, its pretensions were very humble. In consequence of the slender patronage extended to it in its infancy, it was more than five years, as we have seen, after the incorporation was passed, before the business of instruction was commenced. A single building of two stories, now known as the East Building, was the only edifice, and that was occupied in part by the Preparatory School. Two instructors only were employed, and the scale of studies was exceedingly contracted when considered as the course prescribed by a University. Throughout the whole establishment, there was much to try the feelings and exercise the patience of those to whom was entrusted the task of maintaining its discipline and communicating instruction. The population of the country was in general rude and uncultured, to a degree of which one, who has not marked the progress of the change, will find it difficult to conceive. The young men, bringing to this place the sentiments and manners which they received from the associates of their earlier days, were but ill-prepared for that quiet devotion to the pursuits of literature and science, without which, the apparatus of professors and libraries and other facilities for acquiring knowledge, can be of little avail. Among the early associates too of Dr. Caldwell, were some of loose principles and corresponding habits, who threw additional obstacles in his way. For these reasons, the early part of his connection with the University was to him a scene of severe suffering and trial; and he seems at first to have been ready to yield to the promptings of his natural inclination, and to have retired from the turmoils and perplexities of his situation, to the less responsible and arduous, though humbler, station he had left. A record is found on the Journal of the Board of Trustees at that period, of the resignation of his appointment; but he was induced to withdraw it immediately, and to continue at his unpleasant, but honorable post. He then nerved himself with fresh resolution to encounter the difficulties which lay in his path; and, by the exercise of an untiring devotion and unshaken fidelity, aided by a resolution and decision of character, which, though not wholly natural, could not be daunted, he at length brought the unformed mass to a degree of order and respectability, which none can fully appreciate but the associates and successors to his labors. In the formation of his character as the presiding officer of an institution in which were thus met the wildest elements of insubordination, we see a striking illustration of the effects of an unwavering determination to walk in whatever path duty may point out. To those who witnessed the exercise of this character in its full vigor and efficiency, it is scarcely credible, how much it was a formation of the circumstances of his situation, united to a conscientious resolution to make himself useful and honorable in the station he occupied. Yet we have the best reasons for knowing, that, in incipient manhood, he shrunk from every thing like sternness and the rigid enforcement of authority, and was much in the habit of looking to others to determine for him in difficult emergencies. His career at Princeton, it is true, had somewhat broken in upon this gentleness of disposition; but the situation of a subordinate officer of a long established College, was widely different from that of the head of an Institution such as ours was in its infancy, and called for the exercise of very different principles. After seeing and clearly estimating what his new station demanded of him, he shook off every opposing habit and feeling, and gave himself up with a noble resolution, to a faithful and diligent discharge of its duties. How well he fulfilled this resolution, will be attested by many a grateful heart and sympathising bosom throughout our State.

During the first nine years of its existence, no one of the officers of the University was distinguished by the title of President. In 1804, Dr. Caldwell, who had for some time been the presiding officer, and who at all times subsequent to his introduction into the Faculty, had been its master spirit, was elected to the Presidency. He had then been recently married to Miss Susan Rowan, of whom he was deprived three years afterwards by death, as well as of an infant daughter, the only fruit of the marriage. He was again married in 1809, to Mrs. Hooper, who survived him. The limits prescribed for this article, will not admit of any extended detail of the incidents of the period of Dr. Caldwell's life subsequent to his elevation to the Presidency, if indeed it were necessary; but they are best known from their results, so richly scattered over the whole face of our land, and so manifest in the circumstances in which our institution now stands, as contrasted with its feebleness and immaturity when first confided to his fostering care. After the first few years of his Presidency, the reputation of the University, continually advancing, attracted so many students, that the want of enlarged means of accommodating them became very urgent; and the building now known as the South Building, much the most spacious of all we have, and containing most of the recitation rooms and lecture halls, was commenced and prosecuted, for some time, with vigor. But the Legislature having withdrawn the bounty it had before extended, and divested the Trustees of some of the sources of revenue originally assigned to the use of the University, left them under the necessity of suspending the prosecution of this work, and leaving it in a condition unfit for any useful application. Two years longer the inconvenience of narrow accommodations was submitted to; but the still increasing number of students caused the want of the additional building to become more and more pressing. At length Dr. Caldwell, whose interest in the institution was never confined to the faithful discharge of the duties of his peculiar office, requested of the Trustees permission to make an appeal to the liberality of the friends of education throughout the State. Nor did he appropriate to this business, any portion of his time required by his more immediate duties. During the six weeks vacation of the summer of 1811, he visited such parts of the State as were within his reach, and having headed the subscription list with his own name and a liberal donation, he obtained the sum of $12,000. This liberal contribution enabled the Trustees to push the work on to completion and thus to secure that patronage, which, in all likelihood, would have been soon withdrawn, in consequence of actual want of room. This well-timed relief gave a new impulse to the progress of the institution in public favor, until additional buildings were once more needed for the reception of students. But the resources of the Trustees had become more ample, and more sufficient to provide all the required accommodations. Having removed this impediment which so seriously threatened the prosperity, if not the very existence of the University, and having seen it grow up from the humble condition in which he found it, to respectability and usefulness, Dr. Caldwell thought that, without hazarding the interests of the institution, he might now yield to the inclination which had never left him, of devoting more time and attention to study, than the duties of the Presidency allowed him, and accordingly, in 1812, he resigned his situation, and returned to the Mathematical Chair. Apart, however, from the preference which he felt and thus indulged, of devoting himself to the task of instruction rather than of direction and discipline, he was contemplating the execution of a literary labor in which he took much interest, and which remains as a monument of his skill in adapting the details of an abstruse science to the comprehension of the young. We allude to his work on Geometry, which, though not published for some years afterwards, (1822) engaged much of his attention and time during the interval which elapsed between his retirement from the Presidency and his reluctant resumption of it in 1817. The subject is one which, in the ablest hands, does not at the present day admit of much that is strictly original. The most skilful mathematician who undertakes a work of this kind, must content himself with moulding into new forms the materials handed down to him by writers of other times, and with introducing occasionally a demonstration that is new, more lucid, or more direct and brief. The object proposed by Dr. Caldwell in this publication, was to produce a system less extended and tedious than that of *Euclid*, but comprising all the capital propositions of that Geometer, and retaining, throughout his strict and rigid methods of demonstration—an object which he will be allowed by all competent judges to have well and happily accomplished. Upon his resignation of the Presidency, Dr. Robert Chapman was selected by the Trustees as his successor. After holding the office for five years, Dr. Chapman retired in 1817, and Dr. Caldwell was induced to resume the situation, which he continued to hold during the remainder of his life, though not without making efforts to resign it. The distinguished success which attended his labors did not fail to attract attention from abroad, as it excited the admiration and gratitude of the friends of the University at home. In 1816, the Trustees of the College of New Jersey, his alma mater, conferred on him, by an unanimous vote, the degree of Doctor of Divinity. And subsequently inducements were held out to him by at least two respectable Colleges to change his situation; but he clung to our College with a paternal devotion, commensurate with the obligations it owed him; and, with a determination which appears to have been formed very soon after his first connection with it, he resisted every attempt to draw him to a more lucrative appointment.

After his re-appointment to the Presidency, he pursued the even tenor of his way, dispensing intellectual and moral good through all our borders. One event, with its auspicious consequences, will detain us a few moments, before we come reluctantly to that solemn period, when the shadows of the grave began to gather over his bright and beneficent career. The Trustees having determined to add to the facilities for improvement already enjoyed by the students of the University, a Philosophical apparatus, and additional volumes for the Library, Dr. Caldwell, entrusting the temporary supervision of the College to the Senior Professor who deservedly possessed his and the public's entire confidence, visited Europe, in order to direct, in person, the constuction of the apparatus, and the selection of the books. He sailed from this country in the month of April, 1824, and landing at Liverpool, proceeded immediately to London, to accomplish the object of his voyage. After having put the business in a train that promised to lead to its speedy completion, he passed over into France; and traversing that country, by the route of Paris and Lyons, after visiting the Lower Alps, passed through the western part of Switzerland and Germany, and proceeded down the Rhine as far as Frankfort, whence he returned to London. Subsequently, he visited Scotland; and at length returned to this country, after an absence of ten months. The fidelity and skill with which he discharged the trust confided to him by the Trustees, are abundantly attested by the excellence of the apparatus which now occupies our lecture rooms, and by the value of the addition made to our library. But far the most interesting result of his visit to Europe, was the strong feeling excited in his mind on the subject of internal improvement—a subject, which perhaps engrossed more of his thoughts during some of the last years of his life, than any thing else connected with this world. The sound practical views which he entertained on the introduction of this system into our own State, and which are ably and clearly set forth in the numbers of *Carlton*, have commanded the admiration of every enlightened citizen; and the zeal with which he advocated it on every suitable occasion, and long after disease had impaired the energies of his body, must secure him the lasting gratitude of every true friend of his country. It is well known, that the magnificent project of a railroad to reach from Beaufort to the mountains, originated with him, and was advocated with such ability as to have rendered it a favorite measure of State policy with some of the most enlightened and devoted patriots of our land long before his death, and finally led to the construction of the N. C. Central and Atlantic and N. C. Railroads.

The first access of the disease by which Dr. Caldwell's life was finally brought to a close, occurred in 1828 or 1829; after which period, as he states in a note made in 1831, he was never in the enjoyment of good health. Nearly the whole of the six or seven years which elapsed before the termination of his sufferings, was a period of unremitted uneasiness; during a considerable part of it his bodily sufferings were severe, and often, he was the victim of excruciating pain. He seldom spoke on the subject even to his most intimate friends; and having a singular power of subduing and controling his emotions, he would often wear upon his countenance a calmness and serenity, that indicated to a stranger, an enjoyment of the blessings of existence; when, to those better acquainted with him, it would be revealed by some involuntary movement, that this appearance of ease and comfort, was not maintained without a powerful struggle. But the triumph which disease was thus achieving over the body, did not, till the very last hours of his existence, extend to the faculties of his mind, or impair, in the slightest degree, the devotedness of the interest with which he cherished the institution, that for so many years had been the object of his fostering care. It is true, that within the last two years of his life, when acute and unceasing suffering disabled him from taking his wonted share in the business of instruction, he proffered to the Trustees the resignation of his office of President; but it was under an apprehension that he was becoming an incumbrance to the College, and would not be able to make a full return of service for the salary attached to his station. That honorable body with a liberality and feeling of gratitude worthy of them and of him, resisted the attempt made by him to surrender the trust he had received from their predecessors. But to relieve him from the task of instruction, and to secure to him the leisure and tranquility which his age and infirmities demanded, they established an Adjunct Professorship, to provide for his entire withdrawal from the labors of his station. The individual selected by Dr. Caldwell himself to fill this professorship, Walker Anderson, A. M., brought to the filial task, a heart full of veneration and love, and a resolution to fulfil to the uttermost the pious purpose of the Trustees. But though provision was thus made, by the character of the professorship and the disposition of its incumbent, for the entire release of Dr. Caldwell from the business of instruction, he could not be induced to avail himself of the indulgence to the extent proposed, but resolutely persevered, till within three days of his death, in performing as much labor as his fast declining strength was equal to. One half of the ordinary duties of his professorship he reserved to himself, and manifested a settled purpose to abide by this arrangement, by assigning to his adjunct, in addition to the other half, a portion of the general business of the College. Though his frame was racked with unremitting pain, and worn and wasted by sleepless and tortured nights, yet on no occasion, except during an attendance on the Presbytery to which he belonged, and a visit to Philadelphia in a fruitless effort to find relief from his sufferings—on no other occasion did he devolve these reserved duties on his associate, though often and earnestly entreated to do so. "*Sepulchri immemor, struit domos,.*" On the Saturday previous to his death, he retired from the lecture room to his bed, from which he never rose again, but under the impulse of his mortal agonies.

The religious character of Dr. Caldwell was not the formation of a day, nor the hasty and imperfect work of a dying bed. His trust was anchored on the rock of ages, and he was therefore well furnished for the terrible conflict that awaited him. We have seen in his autobiography that he had made religion the guide of his youth; it beautified and sanctified the labors of his well-spent life; nor did it fail him in the trying hour, which an all-wise but inscrutable providence permitted to be to him peculiarly dark and fearful. The rich consolations of his faith became brighter and stronger, amidst the wreck of the decaying tabernacle of flesh; and, if the dying testimony of a pure and humble spirit may be received, death had for him no sting—the grave achieved no triumph. In any frequent and detailed account of his religious feelings, he was not inclined to indulge—the spirit that walks most closely with its God, needs not the sustaining influence of such excitements—yet a few weeks previous to his death, a friend from a distant part of the State calling to see him, made inquiries as to the state of his mind, and had the privilege of hearing from him the calm assurance of his perfect resignation and submission to the will of God. His hope of happy immortality beyond the grave, was such as belongs only to the Christian, and by him was modestly and humbly, but confidently entertained. It was to him a principle of strength that sustained him amidst the conflicts of the dark valley, and to those who witnessed the agonies of his parting hour, a bright radiance illuming the gloom which memory throws around the trying scene. On the evening of the 24th of January, 1835, his terrible disease made its last ferocious assault, with such violence, that he knew that his hour of release was at hand. He gratefully hailed the anxiously expected period, and his house having long since been set in order, he withdrew his thoughts from earthly objects, and calmly looked upon that futurity to whose verge he was come. By the exercise of prayer and other acts of the holy religion which he professed, he strengthened him for the last conflict, and spoke words of consolation and hope, to his sorrowing friends. But death was yet to be indulged with a brief triumph, and for three days his sufferings were protracted with such intensity, that his vigorous and well balanced mind sank beneath the contest. We willingly drop the veil over the bitter recollections of that hour, and take refuge in those high and holy hopes, which were the last objects of his fading consciousness, and which had lent to the long twilight of his mortal career, some of the light of that heaven to which they had directed his longing gaze. To no one who lived at that time, need we tell of the universal and heartfelt sorrow, with which the intelligence of Dr. Caldwell's death was received throughout the State. Multitudes there were, who felt that they had been deprived of a personal benefactor—of one, whose kindness and the value of whose services to them, are more and more valued, as increasing experience points out the worth of those labors which the young can never fully appreciate. The Trustees of the University, more than one half of whom had been students of the institution while under his charge, became the organs of the public sentiment, in the expression of the general grief. Some of them, with *alumni* and others from abroad, mingled in the train of the bereaved officers and members of the College, in committing to the dust all that remained to them of their departed Father. All that remained, did we say? We look around us, and stand rebuked for the desponding murmur. The labors of a useful life, to use the thought of the old stoic, are like things consecrated to God, over which mortality has no power. "*Hæc est pars temporis nostri, sacra ac dedicata; quam non inopia, non metus non morborum incursus exagitat.*" The pure and patient spirit has long since escaped its narrow and tempest-stricken prison house, the wasted form is now resting from its sore conflict, in the blessed hope of a joyful resurrection, but those consecrated acts of his useful life remain with us, to spread their benificent influence through successive generations. It is trite remark to speak of the ever-renewed effects of such an influence; but calm observation and reflection abundantly sanction the warm effusions of our grateful admiration. The benefits received from a faithful instructor and guide of our youth, are not only transmitted to our children, but through our whole lives exert a diffusive influence throughout the sphere in which we move. We may say, therefore, without the fear of contradiction, that the whole present generation of the citizens of North Carolina owe to the memory of Dr. Caldwell, gratitude as well as admiration; and that we are indebted to his agency, directly or indirectly, more than to any other individual, for the very remarkable change that has taken place in the moral and intellectual character of our State within the last sixty years. We speak not only of the fruits of his labors, as a faithful instructor and ripe scholar, though it were not an easy task to estimate their extent. We claim not for his tomb, only the sphere and the cylinder which decorated that of *Archimedes*—we speak of the whole moral influence of his life and labors—as a christian minister, an enlightened and active patriot—as one who conscientiously fulfilled all the duties binding him as a man and a Christian; we claim to write upon his tomb the proud but safe defiance—"*Ubi lapsus?*" The relation in which Dr. Caldwell stood towards a great part of the youth of his day, will justify us in inviting the attention of our younger readers to a brief consideration of the principles of that moral strength, which Dr. Caldwell exerted with such salutary power on all who came within his influence, and in endeavoring to draw from thence some lesson of wisdom or motive to exertion. In allusion to the little knowledge which we possess of the early studies of the illustrious Newton, *Fontenelle* applied to him the idea of the Ancients respecting the unknown source of the river Nile: "No one has ever looked upon the Nile in its feebleness and infancy." But we have been more favored. That magnificent stream which fertilized and blessed our borders for so many years, we have just been tracing up to its youngest and freshest fountains, and it is permitted us to draw from thence, new draughts of instruction and delight. As in his maturer years, Dr. Caldwell was the guide and governor of young men, so, in his youth, he should be their example. They should learn that it was in his early life, that his character, in its great outlines, was irrevocably fixed; that the honest, candid, generous and open-hearted boy "foreshowed the man" who brought to the engagements and occupations of after life, the same ennobling principles.

His example confirms, what the example of thousands teaches us, that it is not by sudden and solitary acts of volition that men prepare themselves to become conspicuous, in either good or evil; but by a discipline commencing in childhood, and continuing through youth far into maturer life. If it may be permitted us to look into the elements of that mighty intellect which has been prolific of such momentous results—into the "*altæ penetralia mentis*" before which we bow with such reverence and admiration—we would say that Dr. Caldwell was not indebted in any extraordinary degree to the bounty of Nature, for the extent and perfection of his large mental acquirements. To patient and persevering industry his youth was indebted for that wide and solid foundation, on which the patient and persevering industry of manhood reared so noble a superstructure. But that which we have ever esteemed the great primary element of his intellectual excellence, was the perfect accuracy which he gave to his every mental acquisition. However slow, a strict regard to this fundamental quality might make his progress appear, it was never sacrificed to the whispers of indolence, nor to the murmurs of impatience. Whatever progress was made, though it were slow and painful at first, the ground was thoroughly conquered, and every outpost fully occupied; nothing was left unfinished to annoy him by the necessity of constant retrospection, nor to impede his onward march by a sense of insecurity and doubt. Nor is the eventual flight of a mind, thus solicitous about the accuracy and perfection of its first movements, less rapid or less elevated than the towering, but unequal essays of what is sometimes called genius. The latter may at times soar to the highest heavens, but it has often to stoop to earth to repair the deficiencies of its early preparation; while the former, having once surmounted the difficulties and dull delays of its lower flight, thenceforward moves in a purer sky—

Heaven's sunshine on its joyful way,
And freedom on its wings.

Nor, while thus presenting his intellectual character, would we lose sight of the great moving principle of his moral character. In one word, the Religion of Jesus Christ gave direction and efficiency to all his varied works. To its claims he sacrificed every conflicting passion and propensity of early youth, and it became the easy habit of his manhood and old age.

It has been supposed by some, that the dignity of manner, sometimes approaching to sternness, which characterized Dr. Caldwell's intercourse with the students of the University, was the result of a corresponding sternness of temper. This injurious thought might be easily repelled by the testimony of those who were admitted to the high privilege of social companionship with him, and who could bear witness to the kind and courteous, though still dignified demeanor, which marked all his intercourse with them. Circumstances, easily understood, imparted to his manner, when brought into contact with those under his charge, a certain degree of reserve; which, however, was greatly misunderstood, if regarded as indicating a want of sympathy with their youthful feelings, or a wish to repel them from communion with him. The brief glance which we have taken at the early condition of our College, and its tempestuous elements, which then needed a master-spirit to subdue and control them, reveals to us the necessity there was for that authoritative dignity and decision of character, which, after that period, so eminently distinguished Dr. Caldwell. In obedience to the law which was the rule of his life—the fitting himself to fulfill, in the best possible manner, the duties of the station in which Providence had placed him—he moulded his temper and deportment to the demands of his peculiar situation; and, if in more quiet times he did not entirely recede from the manner which circumstances had forced upon him, something must be forgiven to the inflexibility of habits acquired upon principle, and continued from necessity through many successive years. But who are they who have brought this charge of sternness against his memory? Those who judge hastily and superficially, not those who had the best opportunities of knowing him They who were brought into the closest contact with him, say that, though hardened vice was ever frowned upon with severity, yet, when ingenuous and honorable contrition was excited, his brow was the first to relax, and his tongue the first to drop the balm of kindness and encouragement.

In his general intercourse, Dr. Caldwell was accessible and courteous, and though in his usual habits, much devoted to study, he relished, in a very high degree, the pleasures of intellectual society. In the various domestic relations of life, he exhibited the kindest and gentlest traits of character; and, with a heart and hand open as the day to melting charity, he was the beloved benefactor of the whole circle in which he moved.

We have endeavored to trace, though with a feeble hand, the incidents of a life so dear to us all, and to unfold some of the traits of that character which has been so long our pride and admiration.